There were no such things as werewolves

Laine's mouth was dry with fear and her heart had begun to pound. She hadn't been serious about investigating werewolves, hadn't believed there was any such thing, but now in the dark...smelling the odor of a wet animal and hearing the half-scraping noise getting closer...

Step by step it was approaching, and now Laine could hear faint, occasional panting. Terror made her tremble. She moved toward the hedge, her step soundless, all her attention on what was coming toward her. She still couldn't see anything, but the smell was getting stronger.

And then everything seemed to happen at once. And unearthly howl, a flurry of footsteps, a shout, and then she was knocked to the ground.

Laine struggled wildly against the weight on her back, trying to free her wrist from the immovable strength of the hand wrapped around it. There was a confusion of other sounds, and then, suddenly, there was nothing....

D0830379

ABOUT THE AUTHOR

Sharon Green, a well-known science-fiction author, is a longtime lover of spooky stories. She puts that hobby to work in *Werewolf Moon*, her second Intrigue novel. Sharon lives in Edison, New Jersey, with two of her sons and her five cats.

Books by Sharon Green

HARLEQUIN INTRIGUE
152—HAUNTED HOUSE

Werewolf Moon

Sharon Green

Harlequin Books

TORONTO • NEW YORK • LONDON
AMSTERDAM • PARIS • SYDNEY • HAMBURG
STOCKHOLM • ATHENS • TOKYO • MILAN
MADRID • WARSAW • BUDAPEST • AUCKLAND

Harlequin Intrigue edition published April 1993

ISBN 0-373-22224-6

WEREWOLF MOON

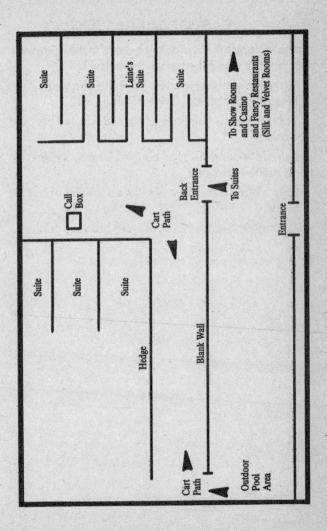

CAST OF CHARACTERS

Laine Randall—She didn't believe in the werewolf myth, but could she ignore the evidence?

Greg Williams—He knew more than he was telling . . . but he told Laine nothing.

Bob Samson—Laine's bodyguard wanted his past hidden.

Donald Meerson—Had his girlfriend seen the mystical werewolf?

Ralph Van Ort—He couldn't stop talking about the beast.

Jeremy Roberts—His eyes were black as coal.

Prologue

"Even a man who's pure in heart
And says his prayer by night,
Can become a werewolf when the wolfbane grows,
And the moon is full and bright."

The Wolf Man with Lon Chaney Jr.

It was the night of the full moon. He stood quietly in the dark, waiting for *them* to come.

He grinned into the shadows that covered him, remembering what he'd left on the ground the night before. Torn and lifeless bodies, covered in blood and looking like rag dolls thrown away by a child. He'd killed before, but under a full moon it felt so right.

The scuff of a footstep in the distance brought his head up, all senses immediately alert. Could that be *them,* the ones he was waiting for? They were his prey and they knew it, but one of his victims the night before had tried to escape. She'd begun to struggle when his claws ripped open her throat, ending all struggle forever.

More footsteps came, now clearly heading for the area of his shadows. They plodded ahead to the rendezvous spot to meet their fate. *He* was their fate, and the eye of the full moon would soon help him accomplish his mission. He licked his lips, letting them get just a little closer...

When he finally showed himself he was all but tasting their blood. Their eyes told him they wanted to run, but it was too late, much too late....

Chapter One

Laine Randall looked around as she stepped off the train, but there wasn't much to see. Elgin, New Mexico, was no more than a whistle stop, dusty, humid and overcast.

"Laine, the conductor would like to have your autograph," Nissa said in a low voice. "I told him I would ask."

Laine glanced at the petite woman who had been with her so long. Nissa Anders was a quiet person, rarely speaking in a voice louder than a shy murmur. But Nissa always knew that it was good press to be gracious to people. Laine made it a policy never to argue Nissa's decisions in the matter, and because of that Laine had a reputation for being one of the nice people in a business that had more swelled egos than a bullfrog convention.

"I'd be glad to give the man an autograph," Laine said in a pleasant voice, calling up the smile that went with that particular role. "Why don't you bring him over?"

Nissa flashed a smile, and then gestured to a short, uniformed man standing about ten feet away with Robert Samson, Laine's very large male secretary. The conductor brightened immediately and began to hurry over, already having dismissed Nissa, who had gotten him what he wanted. People *always* did that to her, and it also always bothered Laine.

"I really appreciate this, Miss Randall," the conductor began babbling at once, his grin the sort that ardent fans usually wore. "You're my favorite actress, and 'Death Beat' is my favorite TV series. You're not only a great detective, you also make a great cop. I hope your series goes on forever."

"Thank you," Laine said with her smile firmly fixed in place, as she took the paper and pen the man held toward her. "Who should I make this out to?"

Victor Bogosian spelled his name carefully for her, then took the completed autograph and reluctantly started walking away. Nissa went to the luggage now standing on the platform, which meant Laine was able to go back to studying her surroundings.

A land where almost all of the life juices have evaporated, Laine thought with a faint, humorless smile, as she surveyed the arid atmosphere of the place. The movie role she'd been offered would be filmed in Elgin and the nearby exotic resort, and if everything went according to plan she would be a superstar.

"Oh, sorry, honey," a male voice said an instant after Laine was jostled by a large, hard body. A big hand had come quickly to her arm to keep her from falling, but the gesture was just as distracting as the words. "Instead of sight-seeing, I should have been watching where I was going."

"No problem, junior," Laine answered in a lazy drawl, and *that* got the man's attention. His head snapped around in the closest thing to an actual double take Laine had ever seen, and his light blue eyes widened just a little. He had tawny blond hair and a square, ruggedly handsome face, but his expression was downright comical.

"*Junior?*" he asked, brows raised high as he looked down at her. "I strike you as somebody who ought to be called 'junior?'"

"At least as much as I qualify for the name, 'honey,'" Laine countered easily, unimpressed by the big man's attractiveness.

"Now *that* point I would have to argue," the big blonde said with a sudden grin, his light eyes moving quickly over her. "You are definitely a 'honey.' If we meet again, we'll have to discuss it over dinner."

He used two fingers to throw her a casual salute before moving off, and made no effort to look back as he disappeared into the wooden depot building. Laine watched him leave, her head to one side, wondering. He obviously didn't know who she was and didn't expect them to meet again, but had made sure to arrange a dinner date in case they did. Distracted interest was what he'd shown, as though he weren't about to let a physical attraction interfere with more important concerns.

"This is *not* the place for *that* look," Bob Samson scolded as he appeared on her right, studying her expression. "That's the 'Hey, there's a mystery going on here that I'll have to investigate' look, and it belongs no place other than on the set of 'Death Beat.' Didn't your producers make that clear through all their yelling?"

"They were just upset because they thought I might have gotten hurt," Laine answered with a grin and a dismissive wave. On three separate occasions she had helped out the Hollywood police department with real crimes. None of it had gotten into the media, but her producers had found out about the incidents and hadn't been pleased. The last case had been the worst, considering how close she had come to having her name added to the list of victims....

"Laine, you may consider the situation amusing, but your producers don't," Bob responded with a sigh. For such a big man he had more patience than most people would expect, and his dark eyes were very serious. "And you may not have been listening to them, but I was. If you get involved in any more real-life trouble, they'll replace you in the series. They weren't joking, so don't fool yourself into believing they were."

Laine nodded with a smile as she patted his arm, hoping he would stop lecturing her if she didn't try arguing again. Bob was a member of her official family, just as Nissa was, and he never stopped trying to protect her, especially from herself. His dark-haired good looks were enough to get him a screen test any time he cared to take one, but Bob didn't want to be an actor. He was studying to be a director, but refused to leave Laine's employ to work at it full time. She needed *somebody* to take care of her, he always maintained.

"If you don't stop trying to push me around, I'll tell Ann you made a pass at me," Laine threatened when his expression didn't lighten much. "You know she tends to believe what I say, so you'd better behave."

"I'm not the one who needs to worry about behaving," he came back with a snort of amusement that at least got rid of the tension in him. "Ann knows I love her, so you go right ahead and tell her anything you like. And while you're considering the best thing to tell her, why don't we go looking for our ride?"

"Did Nissa find someone to take the bags?" Laine asked, turning to see for herself. Just as she'd half expected, the small woman stood near the luggage all alone, without a porter in sight.

"I'll check inside to see if there's anyone here to do it," Bob said with another sigh. He also disliked the way people dismissed Nissa's presence, but every now and then he found *himself* doing it. He shook his head and started toward the depot building, and Laine went back to stand with Nissa.

"Why didn't you tell Bob you were looking at the man and not thinking about a mystery?" the small woman offered shyly, her smile as teasing as it ever got. "Maybe then he would have stopped lecturing you."

"Bob knows better than to believe I would be interested in a man that handsome," Laine returned with her own smile. Nissa always knew what was going on, and as usual was trying to help her. "I've had more than my fill of so-called gorgeous hunks who are dying to be my escorts, but are only interested in what I can do for their careers."

"He looked interested enough to me," Nissa ventured, her smile now dreamy. "I wish a man would look at *me* like that. Just once and I'd be happy, but of course it won't ever happen."

For the millionth time Laine wanted to argue that, but it would have been a waste of breath. In order for Nissa to attract men *she* would have to see herself as attractive. Someone had done a damned good job destroying Nissa's self-confidence.

"Okay, ladies, we can now go looking for our transportation," Bob announced as he came back. Behind him was an old man with a long handcart. "John will give our luggage a ride to the parking area, where the cars from the resort usually wait. If there isn't one there waiting for *us,* I'll have a few words to say to the resort's reservations manager."

"If nothing else, that will teach them a lesson for next time," Laine said with a smile, then watched as Bob helped the old man load their luggage on the cart.

As they waited, Laine, thought about the movie role. She had four days to make up her mind and get back to the producers about her decision. That should be enough time . . . unless, of course, something really interesting happened in Elgin, New Mexico.

THE MAN WHO went by the name Greg Williams moved into the depot building and looked around in a casual way, showing nothing of the faint anxiety he felt or the following relief that washed over him when he spotted the man he'd been shadowing. His quarry was slender and balding and not very tall. Greg knew the man's broken English had given him some trouble as he'd traveled cross-country from New York to New Mexico, but he seemed to have gotten to his destination anyway.

Greg moved confidently toward the arrow indicating resort shuttles, walking only a couple of feet behind the man he was following. He paused to pay the ten-dollar fare, then relinquished his luggage before getting on the van. Greg hoped his reservations had been made, then dismissed the point with an inner shrug. If wires had gotten crossed, he'd take care of it the way he always did.

Once on the shuttle he took a seat a couple of rows behind his quarry, then relaxed as the driver waited to see if anyone else needed a ride to the resort. Greg knew of at least one other person who was going there...

"Hell. That was a *woman,*" he said to himself, a grin on his face as he remembered. He'd been so busy watching his quarry he'd bumped into her, and for a moment she'd actually been able to distract him. No doubt about it, she was a woman who could give him a run for his money.

"That means I've got to get to know her," he told himself firmly. The assignment he was on had top priority, of course, but if his luck held he would need to spend some time acting like an ordinary vacationer. He'd use the opportunity to make sure she took him up on his dinner invitation. He wanted to know more about her, and where she might be found when his assignment was over. It had been a long time since he'd last felt that way about a woman.

He glanced out the window on the far side of the van and saw his black-haired honey near a limo, but she wasn't alone. A small, brown-haired woman and a big man were with her. Greg frowned as he looked at the man, but he knew for a fact that the woman hadn't been wearing a ring. Her male companion might mean trouble in getting that dinner date, but Greg wasn't about to simply give up. He might try and fail, but that didn't mean he wouldn't give it his best shot.

Success. Greg felt himself smile at that, knowing it was what made him so good at his job. He didn't know what would eventually happen with the thin bald man, but so far things had been going well. One of his female co-workers had learned of their quarry's destination, which had led Greg to New Mexico.

Greg had been surprised to learn that his quarry was staying at the Isle of Dreams resort, because the man didn't have a lot of money. That was one of the things Greg had been told by his superiors. His people felt the man was going to pretend to vacation at the resort, but it had occurred to Greg that he might be going there to work. If so, Greg would have been better off trying to get a job there also, but it was too late for that. He'd have to play vacationer even if his quarry didn't, and still try to keep him in sight.

The limo carrying his mystery woman and her friends had already left, and Greg looked up to see four more people get on the van. They were two couples who seemed to be traveling together. The driver got in after them, closed the van's door, and took off.

Greg leaned his head back to enjoy the ride, but thoughts of a bright oval face surrounded by silken black hair interrupted his rest. And she had green eyes, he reminded himself with a private grin. How could he possibly pass on a woman with green eyes?

Chapter Two

The ride to the resort didn't take long. The road they traveled was well paved, and when they reached the place where it forked, their limo driver bore right. Laine wondered where the other road led.

"The other road takes you to a town," Bob supplied, as if reading Laine's mind. "Now we're driving on property belonging to the resort. One of the reasons they built out here was because of the vast amount of land. There's plenty of room for expansion."

Bob knew quite a lot about the resort and the movie because he had agreed to be assistant director on the film if Laine decided to do it, and the producers were very pleased about that. Bob was a detail man who could be counted on, the perfect complement to Keller Farring, the genius director who was already under contract.

Laine nodded to acknowledge what Bob had told her, but was also aware of the facts he hadn't mentioned. The resort wasn't a family hotel, which was what the producers had liked about it. They needed a place with lots of partying. The resort's atmosphere would be a perfect backdrop for the movie.

"I like the way the ground slowly becomes manicured lawn," Nissa ventured, peering out the left-hand window. "It gives the impression of casual opulence."

Laine agreed with the technical remark, but also saw the symbolism. Empty ground slowly becoming a lush lawn, a woman's empty life slowly becoming meaningful. Yes, that fit well enough. Now, if only the rest of the place would turn out as well. . . .

They drove through what looked like a park for a while, at one point seeing people on horseback, and then they reached the hotel proper. Its entrance was as modern and sleek as any expensive hotel, but the building was only three stories high—although it looked as wide as a city block. Two bellmen immediately came outside, and while one opened the door to the limo, the other went to get the luggage out of the trunk.

"Welcome to the Isle of Dreams," the man holding their door said as they began to get out. "We've been expecting you, Miss Randall, and look forward to your visit."

Laine gave the man a smile, enjoying the personal touch. If they did that with every guest who came, they probably got a lot of repeat customers.

Once their luggage was out of the limo, they followed the two bellmen inside. The air-conditioning was an immediate delight, and they were all urged into comfortable chairs while registration forms were brought to them.

"And, of course, you have the choice of eating in one of our fine restaurants, or of having room service," a pleasant young man informed them.

"We'll get settled in our rooms, and then we'll have lunch," Laine told him. "In one of your restaurants," she amended quickly before he asked.

"And then, of course, you may want to look around," he said with a satisfied smile. "There's a map included with your three key cards, but if you'd prefer having a guide just call the desk before leaving the restaurant. Someone will be sent to help you."

Laine thanked him warmly as she got to her feet, then, with a sense of relief, followed the bellman who carried their luggage. Personal attention was all very well, but if she had to hear the words "of course" one more time...

Rather than going to an elevator, the bellman led them outside again. The luggage was transferred to the back of a small vehicle that was open except for the canopy on top, and had seating enough for six. They all got in, and as the bellman drove off slowly they were able to look around at the beautiful little houses to either side of the wide driveway.

"Your suite is 7-R," the bellman said, gesturing to the number-letter combination on the front of the small house they were approaching. "There are two carts available for your use, but if you need another, just ask. If there's anything you need, all you have to do is call."

Laine resisted the temptation to say that the sentiment would make great song lyrics, and the way Bob glanced at her said he'd been thinking the same thing. The bellman, having missed the exchanged glances, simply went to the canopied front door and opened it with the key card he held, then went back for the luggage while they went in and looked around.

"Oh, this is beautiful," Nissa breathed in timid delight. The entrance area beyond the doorway spread out into a beautifully decorated living room, while a hallway to the immediate left—done in Spanish tile— curved out of sight after fifteen or twenty feet. At the far end of the living room was another archway on the left, and Laine wondered if it was the other end of the same hallway.

"If you'd like to choose your bedrooms, I'll put these bags where they belong," the bellman said.

The man gestured up the hallway to the left, so Laine led the parade in that direction. Each of the three bedrooms—complete with private bath—was enormous. Laine took the first room, Nissa the second and Bob happily settled for the third.

While the bellman went back for the rest of the luggage, Laine investigated another door to the outside that stood between the second and third bedrooms. It proved to be the private entrance to their backyard patio, which had a full-size swimming pool and sauna as well as a large table with comfortable chairs. The three of them looked around at the hedge-screened area, and Nissa sighed.

"Wouldn't this be perfect for a honeymoon?" she asked, and then she blushed. "For the honeymoon of someone important, I mean," she quickly amended. "It looks like heaven."

"There's even a shade tree to rest under," Laine said, impressed in spite of herself. "I just may come back here on vacation."

"Ten years from now it may not look as good," Bob commented, not even glancing at her. But just because Laine hadn't taken a real vacation in all the years he'd worked for her, that didn't mean she was *never* going to take one.

"Let's go get lunch," she said, ignoring Bob's remark. "After that I want to look at the main hotel. As appealing as this place is, I do have to be back home in four days."

"You have to give them your answer in four days," Bob corrected in an almost offhand way. "Of course, I'm assuming they have telephones in this place. It might be worthwhile to think about that."

"I have two guest appearances scheduled for next week," Laine stated, then didn't say anything else.

Bob knew she had commitments, but he also knew there were eight days between now and the first of them. Rather than commenting again, Bob gave the bellman a tip and the conversation thankfully ended.

They decided to walk back to the main hotel to have lunch. Along the way Laine admitted to herself that the biggest problem was having no one to go on vacation with. Every prince she had ever kissed had turned into a frog, but that was just the way life was. If she ever found a prince *without* an inner frog she would probably kidnap him, but in the real world that wasn't likely to happen...

GREG FOLLOWED THE BELLMAN into the room he'd been assigned, a richly furnished bed-sitting room on the third floor of the hotel's main building. He knew about the suites available in the areas beyond the main building, but one of them wouldn't have suited his purpose.

Once the bellman had given Greg the standard hospitality speech, he took his tip and left. Greg immediately went to the key card folder and withdrew the map that had been mentioned, but he could see at once that it would only be of partial use. Not everything he would want to see was shown on the map, which meant he had a telephone call to make.

After carefully checking the room for bugs, he did the same with the telephone. Different bugs sometimes registered on different frequencies, and all phones had to be checked. After completing his task, Greg got comfortable in the chair next to the phone table.

He dialed his number and waited for an answer. It came on the third ring the way it was planned, with a simple, "Hello."

"Well, hi there," he responded with heavy friendliness. "This is Greg, and I'm calling to say I got here in one piece. You should see this place. It's so beautiful, I'll probably stay longer than I planned."

"Let's hope that isn't necessary," the voice on the other end said dryly. "When we made your reservations, we also managed to get someone in on the staff. Anita Morrow is there as your backup. Is there anything you need?"

"As a matter of fact, I could use a really detailed map of this place," Greg said. "There were four other people on the van with me and our quarry, but only five of us registered. He was led in a different direction, so I'm guessing our man has a job here. I need to know the places employees are likely to be."

"I'll have Anita get you one," his contact agreed, sounding as though he were making notes. "She'll also have a complete guest list for you, detailing those who are there and those who are due to show up shortly.

Give me your room number, and I'll get things rolling."

"I'm in 322," Greg answered. "I'll wait here until Anita calls, but if she's going to be held up, get back to me. I need to learn the layout of this place as fast as I can, and walking around will accomplish that more than sitting here."

"It shouldn't be longer than ten or fifteen minutes, so just relax," his co-worker advised. "Things will be happening soon enough, so there's no need to rush them."

Greg was about to point out that that was easy enough for someone not on the scene to say, but it really wasn't worth going into. He simply agreed to be patient.

It really was only ten minutes later when a knock came at his door. When he went to answer it, he saw an attractive blond chambermaid standing outside.

"I was told one of these rooms is short on towels," the woman said with a smile. "Have I found the right place?"

"Come on in and let's take a look together," Greg invited, having no trouble returning the smile. Anita Morrow was a good-looking woman, not to mention a reliable associate. Greg had worked with her before, and was always glad to see her.

"I can't stay long, love, but I do have what you need," Anita said as soon as the door was closed behind her. "You're lucky I do maps first thing, or you would have had to wait or do your own."

"Luck has nothing to do with it," Greg returned with a grin, taking the small manila envelope Anita handed over. "I prayed like hell that you would be the one they put inside, and that's what did it. How's life been treating you?''

"Better than I was expecting," she answered with a laugh. "I even managed to meet someone who could turn out to be Mr. Right—if he doesn't break and run."

"Our kind of life tends to make people do that," Greg commiserated with a nod of understanding. "If you figure out a way to nail him down, don't forget to tell me about it. It might be a procedure that can also be used on women."

"Tell, nothing," she came back with a snort of amusement. "If I ever figure out a way to do it, I'll make my fortune by *selling* the procedure to the rest of you. A girl has to think about the future, after all."

"It saddens me to think I'm friends with a mercenary," Greg said so solemnly that Anita laughed again as she turned to the door. "When guilt begins to eat at you, you can get back into my good graces by offering to waive the fee in my case. I won't tell anyone else."

"First there has to be something for you not to tell," she pointed out, pausing to look at him. "If I need to talk to you, I'll leave a message with the desk. If you need *me,* call down for extra towels. I've already made an arrangement with the head of the housekeeping department, who thinks I'll be hitting on any single guest I can attract. And I'll take over watching Rolfe Lundgren for the next shift, to give you a chance to go over that data and play careless vacationer for the rest of the staff. If necessary, be prepared to replace me at eleven."

"Because if the subject decides to go out and play, that's the most likely time he'll do it," Greg recited, then smiled at Anita. "I'm glad to see I trained you so well. You've got my procedures down perfectly, except for one thing—where in all this manicured grass surrounded by desolation would the subject go to play? With a pack of coyotes?"

"Since you're the hotshot on this assignment, *you* figure it out," she returned with a grin. "I wouldn't think of lecturing my superiors. Do enjoy your fresh towels, sir."

Anita left the room with that, taking the towels she'd spoken of with her, and Greg laughed softly as he carried the envelope she'd given him to a comfortable chair. There *was* no place for the subject to go around there, but Anita wouldn't have admitted that even under torture. She'd been trying to show him how efficient she was. Unlike some of their other coworkers, Greg knew exactly how good she was and had no need to be convinced.

But now it was time for him to exercise some of his own skill. He'd have to absorb as much of the data he'd been given as quickly as possible, and then go out to show himself as an eager vacationer bent on finding a good time. Sitting around in his room would make him look suspicious, and if anyone was watching...

Greg laughed again as he blessed his good luck, more than willing to admit he was delighted with the way things had worked out. He would firm up a dinner date with a certain black-haired woman, and doing it would be strictly in the line of duty. After all, she was another guest he *would* be interested in, wasn't she? Going after her could be considered no more than part of his job.

He pulled out the paperwork he needed to study, but first took a moment to consider a battle plan. He had a feeling he would have to work to get his date, so he'd better be prepared.

Chapter Three

"I think we had lunch in the wrong place," Bob commented as he looked around at the latest area they'd peeked into. "Next time we have to try here."

"Oh, I couldn't," Nissa protested with a blush, trying not to look around. "Especially not if you have to wear what *they're* wearing. Oh, Laine, please say we don't have to."

"You know you don't have to do anything you don't want to," Laine answered, glancing at Nissa with amusement. "But if you stop to think about it, all they're doing is wearing togas and having their meals served while they lie on couches. It's the waiters and waitresses who are practically naked—and the ones standing around holding those big feather fans. Don't tell me you've never seen anything like this in Hollywood."

"Only on film, which makes all the difference," Nissa said with a sigh, knowing Laine was teasing her. "Trying to eat in the middle of a Roman orgy would give me indigestion."

"Well, of course it would," Bob agreed soberly, joining in the teasing. "You don't want to *eat* in the middle of an orgy, you want to orgy. Ah—could you

point out where all this orgying is going on? All I see
is eating.''

"Maybe it was in the open-air bathing area we
saw," Laine mused when Nissa blushed harder and
didn't answer. "A separate part for men, another for
women, and a third for those who don't mind mix-
ing. Think we ought to go back and double-check?''

"But we're supposed to go on to the game rooms
next!" Nissa blurted, then closed her eyes with self-
exasperation. She'd managed to forget Laine was just
teasing, and if Bob wasn't chuckling at her naiveté it
was only because he was trying to be nice. She wasn't
the only one who tended to believe Laine when she
said something, but...

"Then let's go on to the game rooms," Bob put in
smoothly, beginning to lead the way out of the unusual restaurant. "I've been wondering what this resort considers games, so the time should be very
educational.''

"They probably consider everything games," Laine
said, taking his attention away from Nissa. The poor
girl had been teased enough for one day, and it was
time to let her slip into the background again. "What
I'm wondering is if there's a difference between daytime games and nighttime ones. This wing comes out
and away from the main body of the hotel, so ceilings
can be transparent or pulled back entirely to give access to the open air. Isn't the major gaming room
supposed to be on the other side of the building?''

"Where everything can be close, crowded and
smoke-filled," Bob confirmed with a nod. "Only with
two tiers of gaming balconies above the main floor, it
isn't close *or* crowded. That one is only open at night,
the map says, and formal attire is de rigueur. Down at

this end you can apparently wear anything you please, if you don't count the togas in the restaurant and the bathing suits on the people at the poolside oasis."

Laine nodded, remembering the giant pool with private nooks arranged around it, open areas for socializing, bar and very well stocked food grill. The area had also been less than completely enclosed, with a cart path leading away from the back right. There had been only a small number of people there, and not because the resort lacked guests.

"Yes, here's the proof you don't need to be all dressed up in order to lose your money," Bob said, gesturing to the two doors he'd been looking through on the other side of the corridor. When Laine walked closer she saw a room with tables through the door to the left, and the people at the four occupied tables seemed very absorbed. "Private card games in a place with its own bar and munchies, and on the right is a much larger selection of diversions. No one in sight, though, is wearing anything fancier than sports clothes."

Through the door on the right was a larger room with more varied games, and along the far wall was a line of slot machines. More people were in there than in the card room, but there was still no overcrowding.

"I think they're playing on credit," Laine commented, peering through the door. "It looks like they're handing over key cards rather than cash."

"An innovative way of keeping track of peoples' credit lines," Bob observed, glancing in over her shoulder. "These must be the folks who can't wait until the big casino opens, which means their credit lines *need* to be watched."

"Maybe they just can't find anything else to amuse them," Nissa offered, her hesitant voice sympathetic. "They don't necessarily have to be hooked on gambling."

"Sometimes, sweet child, you can do more harm than good by giving people the benefit of the doubt," Bob told her gently. "There's a gym for those who want to work out, massage tables and steam rooms for those who don't, facial, body and hair salons, barbers and makeup experts. There's even a fashion show, not to mention classes on calligraphy, flower arranging, painting and dance. If simply sitting around a body of water bores you, gambling isn't your only alternative."

"And that doesn't even count the tennis, handball and racquetball courts," Laine felt compelled to add. "Or the horse, bicycle and cart trails, or the boating on the artificial lake they built. Did you see that cold room where they have ice-skating? It isn't a gigantic rink, but it's big enough to have fun on. There's even a video library, and you have the choice of taking it with you or using a viewing room. It would be hard to name some diversion they *don't* have."

"And this is just the daytime stuff," Bob reminded them both, his expression very neutral. "Don't forget our waiter at lunch hinted that things got a lot wilder after dark. He said something about partying across a terrace of fountains on the second floor, and then he laughed. I wonder if they'll decide to add any of *that* to the script when they hear about it."

"There's already a spontaneous orgy scene that the lead character *doesn't* participate in," Laine reminded him, distracted by possibilities. "It's during a party that gets out of hand, and she's so drunk she almost lets herself be drawn in. The next day she realizes she doesn't even like the people who were there, but she almost shared her body with them. It sends her into a rage of self-disgust.''

And now Laine was wondering if it should *be* rage the character felt. She would be angry, certainly, but shouldn't she also be shaken? If you come that close to something that would normally disgust you, shouldn't there be fear somewhere . . . ?

"Oops!" Laine stopped just short of the large body that had materialized in front of her, finally breaking through her thoughts. She'd been too deep in concentration to see the man approaching up the corridor, and she'd almost walked right into him.

"That's perfectly all right," the man assured her with a grin. "I'm also a believer in getting even rather than mad. But we can talk about that later. I just wanted to double-check that six-thirty is all right for you. If you prefer, we can make it seven."

"What are you talking about?" Laine asked without any attempt to pretend she wasn't lost. She recognized the man now as the one who had bumped her at the station. "What about six-thirty or seven, and what am I supposed to be getting even for?"

"Well, I bumped into you, and now you almost did the same with me," he explained, the easy grin still on his handsome face. "Fair is fair, after all. But what I really came looking for you for was to confirm the time I'll be picking you up for dinner. I prefer six-thirty, but if you insist we can make it seven."

"If I insist," Laine echoed, only partially distracted by the man's outrageous nerve. The rest of her was very curious about why his plans had suddenly changed. At the station he'd had more important things to do than be interested in her, but now she apparently had his full attention.

"What are you up to?" she demanded before she could stop herself. "You know as well as I do that we don't have a date, so what are you really after?"

"I'm an international jewel thief after your fortune in diamonds," he answered at once with a laugh. But had there been a flicker of guilt in those very light eyes? "If you don't know what I'm up to, you can't possibly own a mirror. And we most certainly do have a date. I invited you to dinner when we first met, and you made no effort to refuse. That means acceptance in my book, so what time shall I pick you up?"

"Miss Randall has already made other plans for dinner," Bob interrupted smoothly as he came up on Laine's right. "If that changes she'll be sure to get in touch with you, but right now—"

"Why don't we let Miss Randall speak for herself?" the big blond stranger interrupted in turn, just as smoothly as Bob had. "She doesn't strike me as a lady who needs other people to make decisions for her, so why treat her like a child? She—"

"No one is treating her like a child," Bob broke in to protest, his face becoming a shade of deep red. "She *does* make her own decisions, but I'm here to—"

"Then let's hear from *her* what that decision is," the stranger insisted, still calm and reasonable but completely unimpressed. Bob was somewhat larger than the man, but Laine could see he wasn't bothered by that in the least. "Unless, of course, you're afraid to let her out from under your thumb," the newcomer felt it necessary to add.

"All right, that's enough from both of you," Laine broke in just as Bob was about to rise to the bait again. "If you're looking for an excuse to fight, find it somewhere else. I'll be in the Velvet Room at six-thirty tonight for dinner, and anyone who shows up is welcome to join me. Does that decision satisfy everyone?"

The blond stranger looked only partially satisfied as he walked away, but that was triple what Bob was obviously feeling. Laine's friend took her arm and gently dragged her back to where Nissa waited, then glared down at her.

"Are you out of your mind?" he demanded, working to keep his voice as low as possible. "Don't you realize what you've just done?"

"She's only going to have dinner with him," Nissa soothed, trying to draw Bob's anger away from Laine. "He's such a beautiful man, after all, that you can't really blame—"

"Nissa, she wants to *investigate* him!" Bob all but growled, his furious gaze still on Laine. "She was looking at him with her head tilted to the side, and if you don't know that means trouble, I do! So what do you think he's guilty of, Laine? Mass murder? Treason?"

"Bob, my producers will never find out," Laine said with swallowed amusement, putting one hand to his arm. "I'm only curious, and at the first sign that anything major is about to turn up, I promise to run, not walk, to the nearest exit. I'm not letting him pick me up at the suite, so that should tell you I mean what I say."

"You always mean what you say," Bob came back with annoyance. "It's the fact that you don't always say what you mean that gets me. Why can't you be like other women and simply appreciate a good-looking man without trying to find some mystery attached to him that could end up getting you thrown off the show?"

"It's my real interest in mystery that made the show a success to begin with," Laine couldn't help pointing out. "When my character gets intrigued, so does the viewing audience. And how do you know I'm *not* interested in the man himself? As you and Nissa both pointed out, he's very attractive."

"That's how I know," Bob returned sourly. "You seem to have an aversion to attractive men."

"Well, now we can go back to looking around?" Laine said firmly, putting an arm around Nissa's shoulders. "And neither of you has to worry. I won't get into any trouble."

Bob grumbled to himself with disbelief, knowing Laine still intended to investigate her mystery man. She was sure he wanted something from her...and she would find out what before she left that place.

Chapter Four

Greg walked through the arch that was the entrance to the Velvet Room, the resort's second fanciest restaurant. The Silk Room was the best, but in order to eat there you had to be in formal evening dress. The prices were also higher, even though it was a virtual certainty that the same kitchen cooked for both.

"Good evening, sir," the maître d' greeted him with polite formality. "May I ask whose name the reservation is being held in?"

"Randall," Greg answered with a faint smile. "For six-thirty. Has Miss Randall arrived yet?"

"I believe not, sir," the man responded, marking something in his book. "May I show you to your table, or would you prefer to wait in the bar?"

"The table," Greg said without hesitation, wanting to be there when she arrived. It was already six-thirty, so the lady was late.

He followed the maître d' across the room, hearing gentle music playing in the background. Since the Velvet Room didn't open until six p.m. Greg had expected it to be quiet, and that was just the way he wanted it.

He thanked the maître d' for seating him at a pleasant table almost to one side of the room, ignored the
menu that had been placed in front of him, and let his
gaze touch again the few people who were in the place.
None of them was his black-haired Miss Randall, and
that led him to another question. Would she come
alone—or would her friends be with her?

"She left you guessing on purpose, didn't she,
buddy-boy?" Greg muttered to himself, wryly
amused. He'd deliberately prodded at what he'd
thought would be her womanly pride when her big
friend had tried to brush him off, but she'd had no
trouble seeing through the tactic. Instead of accepting his invitation to prove how independent she was,
she'd turned around and arranged things to suit herself.

And just where did her big friend fit in? Greg stared
at the plum velvet, blue silk and white wood the room
was decorated in without really seeing it. He was remembering instead how angry the big man had been
over the open invitation Laine Randall had tossed out,
undoubtedly because it had gone in Greg's direction.
Greg had waited just long enough to be sure the argument would not go beyond heated words, and then
he'd walked away to let them clear the air without the
intrusive presence of a stranger.

"But what right does he have to lecture her like
that?" Greg muttered, forced to admit he had also
walked away to keep from starting a fight with the
man. The guest list said his name was Robert Samson. The question of what his relationship to Laine
was bothered Greg.

"Are you always right on time?" an amused voice
asked, shattering the private sphere of thought Greg

had been wrapped in. He looked up to see the object of his musings standing right there in front of him, stunning in a smoke gray dress that looked to be made of the softest jersey. It had a high collar and long sleeves, but did no more to hide the unbelievable body under it than the knee-length skirt did to hide legs of long perfection.

Feeling inexplicably like an adolescent who had been caught peeking in a bedroom window, Greg rose quickly to his feet.

"No, I have to admit I'm *not* always right on time," he said, waiting for the maître d' to seat her before sitting again himself. "I save promptness for when it really counts, the present time being a perfect example. If I'd known you'd show up looking like that, I would have been here before they opened the place."

"That sounds boring," she commented with a grin that lit the green of her eyes. "Have you ordered yet?"

"No, I haven't been here long enough," Greg admitted with a sigh. So she wasn't going to let him compliment her, not even when he'd been telling the truth. It came to him then that he was about to have a dinner date like none he'd ever had in the past, and it was a damned good thing he had some time to kill before he had to go back to work. It was already clear he'd need it to pull himself together.

LAINE GAVE her dinner order to the waiter, then studied her companion while he gave his. The mystery man was looking very handsome in a dark silk suit and conservative tie, but it was almost as though he didn't know it. Not once had he glanced at the mirrored wall not far from their table to see his reflection.

"Hey, you," she said softly when the waiter had left to get their drinks. Her dinner companion raised his light blue eyes in response, and she smiled at his perplexed expression. "Ah, then that *is* your name. I wondered why you didn't mention it, but now I understand. It was too obvious to mention."

"Okay, you've got me," he came back immediately with a grin. "'Hey, you' *is* my real name, but for form's sake I sometimes use Greg Williams. If you get tired of saying 'hey,' you can substitute Greg."

"It's kind of you to make things easier for me," Laine said with the same smile. "And what do you do to pass the time, Greg Williams? When you're not at a resort like this, that is."

"You're not playing fair, Laine Randall," he scolded mildly with one finger wagging back and forth. "All the rules say we're supposed to take turns at the question game, and you've already had yours. Since it's my turn, the question is, what happened to your friends? Are they being fashionably late, or eating somewhere else?"

"They didn't feel like dressing, so they're eating in the Cotton Room, where we had lunch," Laine answered promptly, just to get the question out of the way. If the mystery man wanted to play games, she was completely willing. "Since it's now my turn again, let me repeat—what sort of business are you in, Mr. Williams?"

"The answer is actually quite boring, Miss Randall," he answered with an amused smile. "Since I was clever enough to be born into a family with money, I do whatever I please to pass the time. Usually traveling, but I'm currently on vacation from it. Terribly high stress situation, traveling. You worry if your luggage is still with you, whether your connecting flight will be on time—and the horrible sense of déjà vu when you learn you'll be going through Atlanta *again....*"

He shook his head sadly and heaved a sigh, telling Laine that if nothing else, he wasn't an actor. No one above the age of three would have believed him, but it wasn't as if he didn't know that.

"How terribly awful for you," she commiserated, putting a good deal more belief into her own words. "You poor thing, you must be exhausted. How long will you be resting up here?"

"Oh, about a week or—" he began to answer, then realized what she'd done. "Good grief, you're a cheat!" he accused in shocked tones, his finger pointing at her again. "You said that deliberately to slip in an unauthorized question. I'm going to complain to the judges."

"Don't bother," Laine came back with a grin. "After that performance of yours, they're all on *my* side. Are you sure the rules of this game say we can exercise our imaginations whenever we please? It doesn't sound legal."

"Oh, it isn't," he assured her, leaning back in his chair to let the waiter put a bourbon and branch in front of him. Laine had already been given her glass of rosé, which meant he leaned forward again almost immediately. "We who play this game have to be absolutely truthful at all times. So tell me, lady cheat, what do *you* do when you're not on vacation?"

"I'm the star of a television series," Laine answered, staring him straight in the eye. "The series is very popular, so I'll probably continue being that for another season or two at least."

"Now I *am* going to complain to the judges," he said, heavy accusation back in that light gaze, arms folded on the table in front of him. "I freely admit you're beautiful enough to be a television star, but I resent being considered gullible enough to believe I'm having dinner with one. What do you take me for?"

"Now *you're* slipping in an extra question, but I'll answer it anyway..." Laine said with satisfaction. "I take you for someone who really does travel, most likely out of the country despite that Atlanta comment. Nissa *said* you didn't know who I am, and once again she was absolutely right. My series is on a major network, and even people who don't watch it are still aware of it. So what keeps you out of the country so much, Mr. Williams? And why am I suddenly being made a part of your business?"

"Don't tell me," he responded flatly, his expression suddenly very neutral. "You play a private detective on television, and enjoy carrying the part over into real life. It's either that or you're a female member of the Spanish Inquisition."

"You're closer than you know," Laine replied with a faint smile. "And I don't have to carry a part over into the real world to be able to notice things. When we first arrived in Elgin, you were so preoccupied with something that you refused to let yourself be distracted. Now, though, you apparently can't think of anything but *me*. What happened to suddenly make me so appealing?"

"The deal I was expecting to close immediately has developed a few snags," he answered with a sigh, leaning back in his chair again to look at her from under lowered brows. "I realize I could have told you that immediately, but I was silly enough to believe a woman might resent having a business deal be considered more important than her. If you'll forgive me for trying to spare your feelings, I'll be eternally grateful.''

Laine picked up her glass of wine and sipped from it, trying to figure out what it was that made her believe that Greg Williams was still lying. His latest story was reasonable to the point of being banal, and maybe *that* was it, the fact that it was his *latest* story.

"It's just now occurred to me to wonder how seldom you must get asked to dinner simply because you're a bright and beautiful woman.'' Greg's voice interrupted Laine's thoughts, and now he was staring at her with a searching look. "I mean, are all the men you know deaf and blind, to make you feel that no one would want to be with you unless he had an ulterior motive? I find that very hard to believe, but from the way you're acting it has to be true. It's usually known as the 'ugly heiress' complex.''

"I suppose that's very fitting,'' Laine agreed with a nod, considering the comment. "Wanted for what comes with you rather than for yourself. For people in my position it's an occupational hazard, but that doesn't make what I said untrue. When you go through the routine often enough, you learn to recognize it.''

Greg Williams lowered his head and rubbed his eyes with one hand, giving Laine the impression he was very bothered about something. He also seemed to be thinking, and when he finally looked up at her again it was clear he'd made a decision.

"I'm going to say this only once, and there will *not* be a question-and-answer period afterward,'' he told her very softly. "The reason I'm here is not something I can talk about, at least not with any degree of honesty. What I do, where I come from—none of that has any bearing on the fact that I was delighted to be able to ask you to dinner. I honestly hadn't thought I would find it possible. If you can accept that and enjoy the meal, I promise to refrain from being professionally charming. If you can't, I'll have to leave."

He sat back then and simply waited, his silence underlining the point that the choice was hers. Laine felt the urge to squirm like a little girl, all the questions his statement had bred clawing hard at her curiosity. He *was* a mystery man, then, but she'd been forbidden to poke and pry. If she ignored his warning and tried it anyway, he would get up and walk away.

And that brought her to the real crux of the problem. She knew nothing at all about this man, but did she really want to send him away? He was looking straight at her with those very light eyes, making no attempt to influence her one way or the other. Whatever decision she came to would have to be hers alone, and she had the distinct feeling he was no longer lying. He could be anyone at all, including a mass murderer as Bob had suggested, but he'd told the truth about wanting to be with her.

"Do you realize that not asking any questions at all will probably drive me crazy?" she demanded at last, deliberately sounding sour. "You'll have your dinner date, but I'll end up in an institution."

"I never said you couldn't ask questions," he came back with a sudden grin that even warmed his eyes. Folding his arms onto the table again, he continued, "You can ask anything you like, as long as you don't insist the answers be true. Would you like to hear about my château in the Alps?"

"I already know people who have châteaus in the Alps," she said with a smile, raising her wineglass. "Tell me instead about the pleasant little town in the Midwest where you grew up."

"Now that's amazing," he said, his smiling eyes looking into hers. "It so happens I *did* grow up in a small town in the Midwest, and it was . . ."

His voice went on, spinning tales for her amusement, but Laine didn't mind. They were playing pretend on an adult level, which meant it was just for fun. Greg Williams didn't want anything from her beyond her company, making that the first real date she'd had in years. She fully intended enjoying every minute of it—even if he *was* a mass murderer.

GREG DRAGGED THE MEAL OUT as long as possible, but the time finally came when they had to give up the table. He put a hand to the middle of Laine's back as they walked out of the Velvet Room into the corridor, knowing that wasn't really the way he wanted to touch her. He'd had a better time than he'd ever thought possible, but the evening had to end. In less than two hours he had to get back to work, and that wasn't nearly enough time for Laine Randall. He would have given anything for a full night with her. . . .

"Look, it's raining," Laine said as she peered through the doors to the outside. "I wonder how long it's been doing that?"

"It can't be long," Greg answered, joining her inspection of the downpour. "The soil around those bushes hasn't turned to mud yet. Did you want to stay and check out the night life here, or would you prefer having me call a covered cart? If you try walking, you'll be drenched."

"I take it that means our date is over," she said after the briefest hesitation, turning those incredible green eyes on him as she smiled. "Rather than demanding to know why and where you're going, I'll just say I had a wonderful time. Thank you for the dinner."

"My pleasure," he told her sincerely, silently cursing his luck. If only they had met at a different place and time. "Maybe we can do this again, when my calendar isn't quite so full. Is there someplace I can reach you after you leave here?"

Greg was trying to calm any natural nervousness she might be feeling by not asking for her home address, but fate had other ideas on the subject of calm. Without warning two people came bursting in from the rain through the doors they were standing near.

"They're dead!" the terrified woman shrieked. She was sopping wet and holding both her hands to her face. "It killed them and they're dead!"

"Somebody call the police," her companion rumbled. A husky older man, he was also obviously shaken. "My God, I've never seen anything like that, not in all my life. For Pete's sake, somebody call the police!"

By that time a rather large crowd of expensively dressed people had gathered, but Greg was too conscious of the queasy feeling in the pit of his stomach to care about them. He got directions to where the victims were lying "all bloody" in the rain, then forced his way through the hovering crowd. If one of the victims was Anita, he would never live long enough to forgive himself.

The rain was torrential, but Greg ignored how wet he was getting while he searched. Down along the main path to the suites, they'd said, near a covered call box on the left. Not all that far, especially if you were running....

Greg slowed abruptly as he stared, then came to a full stop less than five feet away from the two unmoving bodies on the ground. In the light of the call box he could see they were torn up terribly. Their throats had been ripped out and blood was everywhere. It appeared as if their bodies had been thrown where they lay. As he had half suspected Rolf Lundgren was the male victim, but Anita wasn't the second. This was a small woman, who somehow looked familiar...

"No!" a voice gasped from his right, and he turned in surprise to see a dripping wet Laine Randall at his side. "Oh, no, it can't be, oh, please, don't let it be! No..."

"Laine, what are you doing here?" Greg demanded almost harshly, trying to pull her away from the stomach-turning sight. "Don't look at them."

"Greg, no!" she moaned, refusing to let him move her. "It can't be! Tell me that isn't Nissa!"

He turned to look at the second victim again, then held the woman beside him very tight. The deathly still body on the ground *was* Nissa Anders, Laine's friend.

Chapter Five

Laine sat in a chair in the living room of her suite, wrapped in a blanket against the wetness of her clothes. Hysteria and shock had both passed, leaving a numbed emptiness. There seemed to be police everywhere. With the death scene so close to her suite, the sheriff was using her living room as an operations post.

"It's all my fault," Bob said tonelessly for the hundredth time from the chair next to Laine's. "If I hadn't come back here to call Ann, Nissa wouldn't have been left alone. I knew she had to talk to the entertainment director about a possible guest appearance for you in the Show Room. Why didn't I stay with her, or make her save it for tomorrow?"

Laine heard the tortured words, but there was nothing she could say to ease him. She was thinking that if she hadn't gone alone to dinner with a stranger, *she* would have been there to protect Nissa. The small woman had always been a victim of life, and now she had become a victim in death.

Suddenly Laine couldn't bear just sitting there. No matter whose fault it was that Nissa had been alone, some *maniac* had done the actual killing. She wanted the murderer's blood to be spilled just as Nissa's had been, and that meant they had to catch him. She left the blanket in the chair and her shoes below it, and moved closer to the knots of busy officials.

"...will certainly show the man was killed first ," one older man was saying to a uniformed deputy. "If her blood sprayed to either side of him, some of it must have gotten *on* him. The rain has ruined a lot of the pattern, but his clothing will confirm my guess. It will have her type as well as his own."

"Ain't gonna be fun doin' an autopsy on those two," the deputy said as he made notes in a small notebook. "Old Doc Billy woulda upchucked even b'fore he got started, but maybe the new man's got a stronger gut. Helluva start in the job, though."

"Between you and me, I'm glad *I* won't have to do it," the older man confided. "I don't mind giving my medical opinion at the scene of a crime, but pathology was not one of my better subjects at school. It's also the reason I never became a surgeon."

"But we gotta know what done that," the deputy said with a sigh, then eyed the older man. "You done any guessin', Doc? Not like summa them others, but *real* guessin'? We ain't got time for camp fire stories."

"You just may have to make time, Ben," the older man hedged, now looking very uncomfortable. "I'm not saying I agree with some of the wilder claims, you understand, just that you can't ignore the evidence. Some sort of animal seems to have torn them apart, and that one clear print in that sheltered patch of dirt is from a very large wolf. Whatever conclusions are drawn have to be drawn from that."

"But not that bull, Doc," the deputy protested. "You can't tell me . . ."

The man's voice faded out as Laine moved away, but it was quickly replaced by another.

". . . hired as a second assistant pastry chef, and only just got here today," another rain-soaked deputy was telling the sheriff. "The woman also just got here today, but we don't know yet whether she knew the man. Could be they met out there by accident, could be they planned it."

"When you find out, let me know," the sheriff said in a rumbly voice, looking around at the other men in the room rather than at the one speaking to him. "And tell everybody that the next time I hear any references to silver bullets or wolfbane or any of that crap, I'm going to start suspending the wiseasses saying it. We have enough of a mess here without anyone adding to it."

"Yes, sir," the deputy mumbled, his expression saying he knew his superior wasn't joking. "I'll tell them right now."

The man moved away with enthusiasm, but Laine was no longer interested in him. It was the sheriff she wanted to talk to, and when she moved closer he turned to look down at her. He was a big man with brown hair and intelligent brown eyes, wearing a nameplate that said Stoddard. His accent showed he wasn't native to that area.

"Miss Randall," he said, making the name sound like a pronouncement. "Have you changed your mind about wanting the house doctor? I'll send one of my men—"

"No," Laine interrupted, impatient with the idea of being sedated and put to bed and out of the way.

"What I want is to know if you've made any progress. Have you any idea who killed Nissa?"

"We're not even sure yet *why* she was killed," the man admitted. "Do you know if she knew the man she was found near? Could she have gone out there to meet him?"

"It's possible, but very unlikely," Laine answered, trying not to rule something out simply because she didn't believe it. "If Nissa knew him, they could only have met more than five or six years ago. That's how long she's been with me, and I'm sure she didn't run into him during that time. She had no interest in a life of her own, you see, and spent all her time catering to me. I can see now I should have done something more to change that."

Laine wasn't surprised that she'd found another point of guilt, but there wasn't time right now to dwell on it.

"As to whether or not she could have gone out there to meet him, it can only be true if she already knew him," Laine continued. "She and I and Bob were together constantly after we arrived, and when I went off to dinner Bob was still here. And if Nissa had wanted to meet someone, she wouldn't have had to sneak out into the dark and the rain to do it. If she'd mentioned she had a date, Bob and I would have been delighted."

"Even if that date was with a second assistant pastry chef?" the sheriff asked, his tone casual. "Wouldn't that have been too much like slumming for the confidential assistant of a big star? If she thought you might disapprove—"

"Sheriff, I wouldn't have disapproved if she'd had a date with a *fourth* assistant pastry chef," Laine interrupted in exasperation. "In a pinch, even Elmer Fudd might have suited. Don't you understand that she never dated *anyone?* She was painfully shy around people, especially men, and I spent years trying to change that. Her sneaking out to meet someone doesn't fit the kind of person she was. Tell me if you've found out anything about Greg Williams."

The abrupt change of subject didn't startle the sheriff.

"Mr. Williams also got here today, probably on the same van that brought the victim," he answered. "The deputy who talked to him said he was a friendly fella anxious to help in any way he could. He said you two had dinner until a little after nine, and you were standing near the doors when those two people came running inside with the news. Is that the way it happened?"

"Yes, but you didn't see him," Laine muttered, pushing her still wet hair back with one hand. "When he heard people were dead, he raced outside as though he expected the victims to be his father and mother. Did he happen to mention why he reacted that way?"

"He said he thought the people might not be dead, and he wanted to help." Stoddard's shrug was neutral, accepting a statement he wasn't then able to disprove. "In all fairness, I have to point out that *you* went racing out after him."

"Only because I had the sudden conviction he was up to something," Laine insisted, then gave up that tack for the moment. If she said she'd gone to dinner with the man because she'd suspected him of some nebulous crime, the sheriff would probably have her locked away in a padded cell.

"Well, he has a solid alibi for the time of the murder," Stoddard said with a sigh. "Unless he knows how to be in two places at once—not to mention having a method of instantly drying himself—I'll have to work on the theory that he's not directly involved."

"You said 'murder' rather than 'murders,'" Laine immediately pointed out, her attention diverted. "Why did you do that?"

"Because that's the way this is shaping up," the sheriff admitted, looking her straight in the eye as he spoke. "You said yourself the Anders woman wasn't likely to have known the dead man, and unless I find out different I mean to accept that. The actual murder victim was the man, and your friend was most probably included because she showed up while it was being done. She was killed for no other reason than being in the wrong place at the wrong time."

Laine parted her lips to argue that, but the words just didn't want to come. Nissa probably *had* been on her way back to the suite, hurrying because it had started raining. If she'd called a covered cart instead...

"So the only murder you intend investigating is the murder of the man," Laine summed up after a moment. "Nissa's death was incidental and therefore forgettable."

"If you mean she shouldn't be dead, you're right," the big man agreed gently. "If you're suggesting her murderer will go unpunished, though, you're flat wrong. When we find out who killed the man, he'll be charged with her death as well."

"But only to make the case neat and tidy," Laine said, letting her bitterness show only in her words. "We wouldn't want any loose ends left untied. No, it's all right, Sheriff, I understand completely. Thank you for explaining your position.''

She turned and walked away before Stoddard could interrupt the way he'd been trying to do, more than aware of how impossible it would be to change the man's mind. He and his deputies would be looking for the person or persons who murdered the man; if Nissa was to be remembered at all, it would have to be done by someone who had known and loved her.

GREG WILLIAMS had stood around in wet clothes in order to be available to answer police questions, so it was only reasonable that when they were through with him he would go to change. He had even made sure to mention that that was where he was going, and had gotten official permission for his departure.

"Which means I'm such a good boy I deserve a gold star," Greg muttered under his breath as he took the elevator up to his room, an elevator he luckily had all to himself. Half the people in the hotel were trying to get as close to the murder scene as possible, while the other half were too interested in their own affairs to be bothered.

But he was bothered. Not only had his assignment suddenly come apart in his hands, Laine Randall had somehow become a part of it. How in *hell* had that friend of hers gotten snarled up with Lundgren? Had she been there by coincidence, or because Laine Randall, her friend and employer, had been busy doing something else and needed a stand-in for the rendezvous?

Greg was up to snarling under his breath by the time he reached his room, but when he opened the door to find Anita inside he got a better grip on his temper.

She was looking absolutely miserable, a feeling he could empathize with only too well.

"Unless you're the one who killed him, you have no reason to look so upset," Greg told her as soon as he closed the door. "Or hasn't it occurred to you yet that the second dead body could have been yours? Come on, Anita. Pull yourself together and bring me up to date."

"Why...no, I hadn't thought about me being killed as well," she answered with surprise, beginning to come out of her distress as Greg had hoped she would. "I've been too busy cursing myself out for looking away at the wrong time."

"If it was possible to know beforehand that it was the wrong time, then you would have something to worry about," he soothed her. "You can give me a rundown while I change out of these damp clothes."

"When I saw how wet you'd gotten, I brought extra towels with me," Anita said, watching him go into the bathroom and turn on the light. "I was in the fringes of that crowd, but I wasn't the only employee there, so no one should have noticed."

"This is one time when I agree with you," Greg said, the words slightly muffled by the sounds of undressing. "Normally only dead men would fail to notice you, but tonight only dead men would *be* noticed. How did you lose Lundgren?"

"He was in the employees' lounge, and had just settled down to watch a video from the library," she answered, smiling to herself at the way Greg was acting. He knew how low she was feeling, so he flattered her to boost her out of it. "I sat there with my own video until he settled down, then decided I had time for a quick trip to the ladies' room. I was gone only a minute or two, but when I came back he wasn't there."

"I think I'm going to have to send a memo to our superiors," Greg said, reappearing with a towel wrapped around his middle while he used a small one on his hair. "If they can't get Mother Nature to time her calls better, they can't complain when someone disappears on us. Did you go right after him?"

"When I checked, his video was still in the player," she answered with a shake of her head, trying not to stare at Greg. He was beautifully built, with light hair covering that wide, well-muscled chest. What a shame they had become such good friends ... "I had to consider that he might have gone for a quick trip to the men's room, and intended to come right back. I gave him three minutes, then went for a walk around the employees' area."

"Was that before or after the rain started?" Greg asked, staring at her thoughtfully.

"Before, but not very long before," she answered with a frown. "It was obviously about to rain, but just hadn't started yet. Why do you ask?"

"I don't know yet," he returned, shrugging his shoulders. "For some reason the timing on this murder bothers me. Go on with what you were saying."

"Well, I checked the area as thoroughly as I could, stopping back at the lounge a couple of times, but Lundgren had disappeared. I even tried the room he'd been assigned to, but only his roommates were there. I was strolling through the main part of the hotel, hoping I could spot him before trying outdoors, when I heard the commotion. The rest I think you know."

"Unfortunately," he agreed with a grimace. "Something must have happened to make them dispose of Lundgren, but I'll be damned if I know what. We need to get a look at the possessions he brought with him."

"I did that after I left you this afternoon," Anita said, relieved that Greg had turned away to get dry clothes. It was much easier to be his friend and co-worker when he was fully dressed. "Lundgren was being shown the kitchen, and his roommates were still on their shifts. I went through everything in the bag he hadn't yet unpacked, and even checked the bag itself. Nothing was there that shouldn't have been."

"The first chance you get, make a list of that nothing," Greg ordered as he carried the clothing back into the bathroom. "The police will gather his possessions and list them, and I want to be able to know if anything's missing. And keep your ears wide open, just in case someone gets nervous enough to say the wrong thing. If you hear *anything* strange, and I do mean anything, let me know right away."

"Will do," Anita agreed, getting out of the chair she'd been sitting in. "You'll be poking around in public, I take it, as a Good Samaritan who was almost first on the death scene. Will Laine Randall be with you?"

Anita expected a brisk answer to that, but she didn't get one. The silence dragged on for a very long moment, and then Greg, wearing nothing but designer jeans, was in the doorway and leaning against it.

"I honestly don't know," he said finally, for all the world sounding like an uncertain schoolboy. "The second victim was her friend, and I need to know why the woman was out there with Lundgren. And whether or not Laine had dinner with me to keep me occupied while a deal went down."

"You had dinner with her?" Anita asked, her brows high despite the very good opinion she had of her co-worker and friend. "You really *must* have a killer technique, as our female associates are always saying. How did you swing it—and why?"

"I took advantage of having run into her at the train station," Greg answered, a slight blush appearing on his cheeks at the teasing. He didn't need any particular technique to get women to go out with him, and Anita knew it. "Since I needed to establish myself as an innocent guest, I asked a very attractive woman to have dinner with me. I didn't know who she was at the time."

"But now you do, and you're suspicious," Anita said, narrowing her eyes as she inspected him. "But not just suspicious, you're also upset. Was the date *that* much of a success?"

"What difference does it make if she was only using me?" he asked quietly, those light blue eyes looking straight at her. "After we saw the bodies I took her to her suite, and her boyfriend all but slammed the door in my face. I didn't have to wait long for the police to get there, but the deputy who questioned me made me feel as though someone had said something to point a finger in my direction. That could very well have been her, trying to keep me too busy answering questions to notice how she was diverting suspicion from her own trail."

"I'm afraid there's something to be said for her being involved in all this," Anita grudged, hating to hurt Greg. "Control had news for me when I checked in with them, all about the heavy money shift currently going on on the West Coast. Someone is getting ready to buy something very expensive, and everyone is trying to figure out what."

"That's what following Lundgren was supposed to tell us," Greg reminded her with a disgusted shake of his head. "Now that he's gone from the scene, we have to try to locate another lead. Tell Control, that to start with, I need background checks on all the staff members. I'll write down the names of a few of the guests that have drawn my suspicion. If they come out clean, then, if need be, we'll go through everyone here."

"And you want them yesterday," Anita added with a nod, knowing the man she was working with. "What about Laine Randall? Would you prefer to have me check her out?"

"No, I intend taking a closer look at Miss Randall myself," he answered, and there was anger in those light eyes now. "If she set me up—well, she'll regret it."

"That I never doubted," Anita murmured. Then she went back to business. "I'll put in that call to Control, give them my report and your requirement and then I'll make that list. I'll bring it by here later, and leave it in your luggage if you aren't back."

"Thanks, doll," Greg said in the middle of turning away, then turned back to grin at her. "Excuse me. I should have said, 'thank you, valued associate.' I'm not trying to start a war."

"Oh, don't worry about it," Anita dismissed his apology with a wave. "We've been friends too long for something like that to be a problem. See you later, sweetbuns."

Greg had to laugh. As Anita quietly closed the door behind her, he reminded himself that this was the second time he'd lost in an exchange of cutesy names. It might be smart of him to give up using them entirely...

And then his amusement disappeared when he remembered who had bested him the first time. Laine Randall, who had turned out to be so much more than just a beautiful woman. She was bright and alive and full of mischief, the sort of woman he'd be willing to climb mountains for—but she could also be something else. His job demanded that he find out what, but he'd also be doing it for himself.

And he'd be doing it tonight.

Chapter Six

"I hope that was the last of them," Bob said from the archway to the hall, referring to the latest police personnel leaving.

"The last of them for now," Laine corrected from the deep chair where she sat cross-legged, her tone thoughtful. "They'll be back as soon as they figure out what direction to take."

"What do you mean, what direction to take?" Bob asked, coming to sit in the chair opposite hers. "You of all people should know how standard police procedure is in something like this. They'll look around for people who had motive and opportunity, and once they have a list they'll start eliminating."

"By checking on their access to means," Laine said with a nod, then showed him a faint smile. "That part of it should be easy. There can't be too many people around here with access to a werewolf."

"A werewolf," Bob echoed, feeling as though he'd been hit in the face with a plate of spaghetti. "You've decided Nissa was murdered by a werewolf? Well, at least that's settled. We'll go back to work first thing in the morning."

"*I* haven't decided anything one way or the other," Laine corrected again, her voice sharper this time. "The werewolf theory comes from the sheriff's men, but he doesn't agree with them. He disagrees so strongly, in fact, that he's threatened to suspend the next deputy who mentions the idea."

"But that has to mean he's afraid it's true," Bob protested, now feeling sick to his stomach. "Laine, what in hell is going on here? There are no such things as werewolves."

"So I've heard," she returned, then unfolded her legs to stretch them out in front of her. "As to what's going on, I'll give you the answer as soon as I figure it out. First thing tomorrow, check on whether tonight was the first night of a full moon."

"You can't be serious!" Bob exclaimed, distantly wondering if he would ever get back to talking normally. "You can't investigate a *werewolf*, not when you've been warned against investigating anything at all! Laine, your career will go right down the drain! Let's go back to checking locations for the movie, so that when the police release us we can—"

"Just forget about Nissa and continue with our own lives?" she flared, leaning forward to glare at him. "Bob, Nissa was closer than a sister to me, and they've already dismissed her death as being 'incidental' to the murder of that man. It's *his* murderer they'll be looking for, *his* ending they want to punish. I'm going to find out who killed *Nissa*, and when he's caught, it will be because he attacked *her*."

"You're really determined to throw away everything you've worked for," he said, seeing the truth of that in her blazing green eyes. "Your producers won't care why you disobeyed their demands, only that you did. Nissa wouldn't have wanted this.''

"I know," Laine said, looking more determined than he'd ever seen her. "That's why I'm doing it. And it's also necessary. The sheriff can't investigate the possibility of a werewolf without looking foolish, but I can. You know, the scatterbrained actress trying to pretend she really is a detective. If I walk around asking about long-fanged wolves, someone could get overconfident and make a slip."

"As long as there really aren't any such things," Bob said, looking at her from under lowered brows. "I know you won't find anyone to admit believing werewolves really exist, but are you sure we're not kidding ourselves?"

Laine stared at him for a moment, hearing the rain outside strike heavily against the windows. Only that and the soft sound of the air conditioner broke the thick silence, bringing her the urge to shiver.

"You're just trying to scare me," she accused at last, a deep breath helping to break the mood. "It won't work, Mr. Samson, so give it up."

"I wish you would tell me what *does* work with you," he came back with the same lowering stare. "Do you do things like this just to aggravate me, Laine? To make me old before my time? I wish I could walk away and let you take your medicine alone, but I can't. Try to get some sleep, and I'll see you for breakfast."

He got up and left the room, and a moment later Laine heard the sound of his bedroom door closing. She knew Bob would never desert her, she thought with a sigh. He would nag and plead and maneuver to get her to do what he saw as right, but if none of that worked he would just shake his head and continue to stand beside her. She had become his greatest burden in life, but even firing him would have done nothing to help. He would still be there for her, no matter how far off the beaten track she traveled.

And this time she was out of the rough and into the deep woods, she realized with a frown. Chasing werewolves was insane, even if there *was* no such thing. Or maybe especially if there was. A really good detective accepted everything in the way of evidence for a working hypothesis, and only later eliminated what was patently impossible.

A soft bump came from somewhere in the suite, probably from Bob's room as he got ready for bed. Still, Laine felt a shiver go through her, and despite the cream-colored sweater and brown slacks she wore, she felt cold. Why did all of this have to happen to sweet, harmless Nissa?

Laine could almost hear Nissa's shy giggle, and the pain she felt brought tears to her eyes. She would catch Nissa's killer. That she swore by everything she held holy, and the vow would stand no matter who—or what—turned out to be guilty.

It took a few minutes for Laine to wrestle her emotions back under control, and then she silently admitted she'd be smart to go to bed. The day had been long and horribly trying, and tomorrow she would need to be sharp and alert. She stood up and stretched to ease the crick that had taken residence in her back, then headed for her room.

She had already closed the door and was halfway to the bathroom, when she realized the room wasn't empty. She whirled around with the intention of hurting whoever was there, but then she saw him where he sat in a chair with his long legs crossed at the ankles.

His fingers were laced behind his head in an attempt to make him seem relaxed, but Greg Williams looked more than ready to take on any blows that came his way.

"What are you doing in here?" Laine demanded, anger suddenly rising very high. He'd changed into jeans and a light blue shirt, but his black jacket and blond hair still looked wet.

"I came to see if you were all right," he answered at once, then seemed to be annoyed with himself, as though he'd meant to say something else. "I mean, you *did* have a bad shock tonight."

"Most people knock on the door and wait to be let in," she pointed out, making sure her own expression couldn't be read as easily as his. "But that's right, I forgot. You aren't like most people, are you?"

"Meaning what?" he asked, bringing his arms down as he stared at her. "That I'm easier than most people?"

"In a way," she agreed, having no idea what *he* meant. "With most people you have to wonder what moves them, but with you I already know. You went rushing out into the rain to look at the bodies because you knew the man."

He stared at her with an almost comical expression as he slowly got to his feet, and then he was shaking his head.

"You can't mean you believe *I* had something to do with the murders?" he said at last, practically in ridicule. "Has it slipped your mind that you and I were together at the time?"

"Yes, together for too *long* a time," she returned, feeling her chin rise. "And then, suddenly, the date was over. Tell me, Mr. Williams, was that because your purpose had already been served? Were you eager to find out if things had gone as planned while you established an alibi? Don't think I didn't notice how neatly you sidestepped the police's question as to whether you knew the man.''

"But I *didn't* know him,'' he protested, now looking annoyed. ''I was in the same van with him coming from the train station, but we never even exchanged a nod of greeting. You, on the other hand, did know the woman, and not just slightly. If anyone was establishing an alibi with that meal, it certainly wasn't me.''

"If you're trying to say *I'm* the one involved in all this, I'm forced to point out how lame a ploy that is.'' Laine smiled faintly, mostly to hide her anger but also to goad him. "I'm not the one who refused to say what he was up to around here. But in a way you're absolutely right. As of a few hours ago I'm very much involved, which you'll learn when I expose you for what you are.''

"You're going to expose...'' he began with brows raised, and then, very suddenly, he was frowning. ''You can't mean you intend poking around in the murders,'' he stated very flatly. "If you really are innocent, that's the worst thing you could possibly do.''

"Where you're concerned, I'm sure it is,'' Laine returned, still giving him that faint smile. "I'm going to prove the hand you have in this is bloody, Mr. Williams, and nothing you can do will stop me.''

"If that's the sort of dialogue your show has, I'm glad I missed it,'' he came back, the words and his expression equally sour. "Don't you realize that if I *was* guilty, you just gave me an excellent reason to add you to the victim list?''

"Go ahead and try it," she invited, making very sure not to look too eager. "I've learned how to take care of myself, so I'm not afraid of you. But you, I think, will learn to be afraid of me."

"I think I'm already afraid of you," he answered with a sudden grin that warmed those light eyes. "You look just as good in a sweater and slacks as you did earlier in a dress, and a woman that appealing has always scared me. Promise me you won't do any amateur investigating. If anything happened to you, the world would never forgive me."

"Is there something wrong with your hearing?" Laine demanded, not the least bit off balance from his sudden change of attitude. "I said I'm coming after you, but not to play fun games. Save the charm for someone who doesn't know you for what you are."

"Why don't you save the acrimony for when you find out what that is?" he countered, all amusement gone as suddenly as it had appeared. "It really isn't fair to get down on me until then. But I wasn't joking. Snooping around where you don't belong can cut your career short the hard way. If anything comes up that you need to know, I'll be sure to come by and tell you."

"How utterly thoughtful of you," Laine couldn't help saying very dryly. "If you're not in the mood to attack someone, your visit here is over. Good night, Mr. Williams."

"Yes, I think I'd better leave before I *do* attack someone," he growled, those light eyes very hard. "Good night, Miss Randall, and I hope you're not too thickheaded to take my advice. It's meant for your own good."

He turned away immediately, and flames of fury made Laine see red. She always hated to have something done "for her own good," and that phrase coming from her chief suspect was doubly irritating.

She followed behind her unwelcome visitor, seeing him leave through the door to the pool area. That was probably how he'd come in, in spite of the fact there was no easy way out. He'd come in unseen—and all but unheard—and had left the same way.

Laine made sure the door was locked, then went back to her bedroom. Greg Williams was awfully good at getting in and out of places unnoticed, which simply increased her suspicion of him. The next day she would have to take some positive action, showing that his threats hadn't scared her off. If she bothered him badly enough, he might lose some of that obnoxious cool and do something stupid.

"More stupid, that is, than give me advice," she muttered to herself as she reached the bathroom. "I don't take advice from lowlife vermin, and tomorrow Greg Williams will find that out."

The promise made her feel better, and she had no trouble at all forgetting how pleasant dinner with the man had been.

GREG GOT WET AGAIN going back to the hotel building, but this time it didn't bother him as much as it had going out. He was too involved in trying to make up his mind about the conversation he'd just had with Laine. He wasn't used to a woman who was so hardheaded.

There was a small lounge off the well-filled Show Room, and Greg took a booth in the darkest corner and ordered a drink. He'd had to climb through a hedge wall to reach Laine's suite without being seen and noticed by several people still staring and pointing at the death scene.

He tried to lure himself into thoughts about how ghoulish some people could be. But his mind was still on Laine Randall, and how his decisiveness turned to mush when she was right there in front of him. He'd carefully planned his conversation with her, so that he could take advantage of her shock at his unexpected appearance . . .

But things didn't go his way. She'd turned those green eyes on him with pain-filled fury blazing out, and all he could think about was whether she was all right. He had seen the tracks of recent tears on her face, and would have bet every cent to his name that she hadn't cried until *after* the police were gone.

"Which makes you a double-dyed imbecile," he muttered to himself, wishing the girl would get there with his drink. "Or do those beautiful green eyes make you forget she's a professional actress?"

And that, of course, was where the heavy indecision came in. He ran a weary hand through his rain-wet hair, trying to make up his mind about her sincerity. Was she really an innocent bystander who seriously thought *he* was guilty, or was she an extremely clever woman turning away all possible suspicion? He knew which one he *wanted* her to be, and that was the biggest part of the problem.

"Did you say something?" the waitress asked as she set a glass down in front of him. "If you were talking to me, I'm afraid I didn't hear you."

"No, I was talking to myself," he told her with a smile, putting a five-dollar bill on her tray. "I have woman trouble, and a man with that kind of problem often talks to himself.''

"If she's giving you trouble, she's a fool,'' the girl returned with a grin to thank him for the tip. "If you get tired of talking to yourself, come and talk to me instead. Just ask for Mardra.''

Mardra was a beautiful girl and knew it, but Greg wasn't even seeing her as she walked off with a swing to her hips. He was remembering the way a woman with black hair was telling him she knew him for what he was. Those were the exact words Eve had used, and they still had the power to hurt.

"You know Laine will react like the others, so why is this such a problem for you?'' he muttered to himself.

He wasn't able to answer that, but the uneasy feeling that gripped him still refused to go away. He wanted Laine Randall to be innocent, and he wanted her for himself.

"So we'll take it one step at a time,'' he told the glass as he raised it to his lips. "First we'll find out for certain if she's innocent, and then we'll go on from there. But even before that we're going to finish this nice stiff drink.''

Which he proceeded to do. It had come to him that if she *was* innocent, she might actually try to investigate the murders. He'd never allow that, of course, especially if she was innocent. To stop her, he'd . . .

Chapter Seven

The next morning was warm with bright sunshine, which Laine appreciated while she had breakfast with Bob on their back patio. The world smelled fresh and alive rather than dead and filled with grief, and Laine was determined to take advantage of the encouragement. She made lists while she ate, and Bob took the silence as long as he could.

"I hope that's a shopping list," he said at last, holding his cup with both hands in an attempt to look casual. "Actually, I'd even settle for a list of tourist attractions."

"You must be really desperate," Laine returned with an involuntary grin, glancing up at him. "The last I heard, you rated visiting tourist attractions two steps below moving an entire household every year."

"And moving every year should be the punishment for mass murder," he agreed with a grimace. "That doesn't mean there aren't worse fates, so what are we scheduled to see first?"

"This is not a 'see' list," she told him, staring at the page to figure out what was missing. "This is a 'do' list, and it belongs to both of us. As soon as we're through eating we'll get started."

"I have a feeling this is going to be a very hungry day," he observed, sipping his coffee. "I may not stop eating until I go to bed tonight."

"You'll get fat," Laine countered back, then added, "But if you don't want to help, I certainly won't force you. I'll just do it all myself."

"Have I told you lately what a brat you are?" he asked with a pleasant smile. "What do you want me to do?"

"I want the pot to stop calling the kettle black," she answered with a snort. "You can outbrat me any day of the week, and I think we both know it. The first thing I want you to do is call Lieutenant Halloran at his Hollywood precinct office. He was very grateful those times I helped him out, and now I'd like a favor in return. Tell him what happened here, and ask him to call Sheriff Stoddard in his official capacity."

"To ask the sheriff if he'd be kind enough to share his findings with you," Bob said with a sour nod. "I was wondering if you'd try to get official cooperation. What if he refuses?"

"Which one?" Laine countered. "If Lieutenant Halloran refuses, thank him anyway, then let slip I intend calling his captain personally. His captain wanted more than an autograph from me, and would love to have me owing him a favor."

"And Halloran can't stand his captain," Bob acknowledged with another nod. "On top of that he feels protective toward you, so he probably won't let you go to his captain. Doesn't it bother you to use people like that?"

"No," she lied, looking down at her list again to avoid the accusation in his eyes. "I'll do whatever is necessary to find Nissa's killer, and using people will

probably be the least of it. If the sheriff refuses to cooperate, tell him I intend pursuing this werewolf business. That way he'll have the matter looked into
without having to take official notice of it.''

"Which should appeal to him," Bob commented.
"I'll call Halloran, and then we can conference the call
to Stoddard. What do I do after that?"

"First make sure the sheriff sends over copies of
whatever he has so far, and then check on that matter
of the full moon. If the moon *was* full, find out how
many more nights until it starts waning.''

"What about the silver bullets and the wolfbane?"
Bob asked, his tone so serious Laine looked up at him
in surprise. "Do you want me to order them *before* I
make the calls, just to be certain they're in stock? If we
have to wait until they get sent from a distributor, it
could cause a delay.''

"We'll be going ahead with or without them,"
Laine said, hating the way he was using his sarcasm in
another attempt to frighten her. "If we find the werewolf before the stuff comes in, we'll have to impro-
vise. After the telephone calls, you can walk around
shaking hands with people.''

"Why?" he demanded in confusion, disliking the
way she'd ignored his very unhelpful attitude.

"Really, Bob, where's your mind today?" she
asked, lifting her own coffee cup as she stared at him
with a neutral expression. "Shaking hands with people will give you a chance to check palms for the sign
of the pentagram. You know, the sign that the person
you're talking to is a werewolf.''

"Oh, right," he acknowledged, leaning back with
a return to sourness. "It's been awhile since I last saw
the movie. But doesn't seeing the pentagram mean

you've been tapped to be the werewolf's next victim?''

"I'm not sure I remember," Laine said thoughtfully. "If it does, though, and you see it, we've got it made. We'll be able to grab the beast when it makes its try for you."

"That means you'll need a pair of silver handcuffs, too," he said with a nod, as though adding items to a mental list. "*That* I can probably swing, but you have a serious problem to consider. What language do you Miranda a werewolf in? If you use the wrong one, he could get off on the technicality."

"Not if I let him tear you into little pieces while I cheer him on," Laine pointed out, making no effort to hide her annoyance. "Then I can use my trusty silver bullets to shoot him down in the act, and Miranda won't apply. If you really don't want to help, Bob, just say so. The last thing I need right now is you needling me."

"No, the last thing you need is to forget how dangerous this could turn out to be," he countered, angry now. "How will it help Nissa if you end up on a morgue slab next to hers?"

"It won't, so that means I'll have to stay off the slab," Laine said, then leaned forward to touch his hand. "Bob, you have my word I'll be careful, but this is something I *have* to do. Please don't worry about me."

"Sure, I'll stop worrying right after I get my blood to stand still in my veins," he answered with a sigh, patting her hand with his own. "If you're that determined to age me before my time, let's get on with it. If you stop to think about it, there's something peacefully attractive about a porch and a rocking chair.''

"And I'll see you get them as soon as we're home,'' she promised with a grin. "I'll even buy you a nice shawl with matching lap robe for your birthday, but only if you get to those calls before your voice weakens. I have to know what solid evidence the police have before I can even begin to eliminate possibilities.''

"Never let it be said that I'd stand in the way of your eliminating possibilities.'' Bob finished his coffee, but still didn't rise to his feet. "And what will *you* be doing while I'm slaving away over a hot telephone?''

"I have to make a pest of myself among the other guests, but I can't really start that until this afternoon,'' she answered, back to frowning at her list. "Too many people at a place like this don't show their faces until lunch.''

"Thank God for that at least,'' Bob muttered, then held up a hand to keep her from speaking. "Don't throw me to the werewolf again, it was nothing more than an involuntary utterance. If your act won't start until later, why don't you come with me while I make the calls? That way you'll be right there if I need you.''

"You won't need me,'' she said, knowing that for a fact. "Besides, I'll be spending this morning playing rough shadow.''

"With who?'' he asked, beginning to look worried again. "And if I'm not mistaken, it isn't supposed to be done alone. The rough shadow lets the suspect see he's being followed to rattle him, but when the rattling works and the suspect tries to lose the shadow, another person or team takes over. You don't have…''

"Bob, where is the suspect going to take off to?" she asked as reasonably as possible while she finished her own coffee. "If he tries to leave the resort, the sheriff's men will grab him. If he stays here and tries to tough it out, he could get rattled enough to make a mistake. That's the possibility *I'm* hoping for."

"Why doesn't that surprise me?" Bob said with exasperation. "If it isn't dangerous, you're not interested. And you still haven't told me who."

"My target is Mr. Greg Williams," Laine supplied with grim pleasure, getting to her feet. "Want to bet I won't have him climbing walls or hiding in a closet by lunchtime?"

Bob didn't take the bet as he watched her walk away, but not because he thought he would lose. He didn't know much about Williams, but the day before, he'd seen enough to wonder if Laine had finally met her match.

Bob shook his head as he stood, trying to decide if he should worry. He hoped Laine wouldn't push the man too hard, but at the moment there was nothing he could do. On the other hand, if Mr. Greg Williams harmed Laine, he would move as swiftly and cold-bloodedly as Nissa's murderer had...

GREG SLEPT LATER than he'd expected to, and not just because he'd gotten to bed late. He'd awakened with a pillow held tight in his arms, and even if he hadn't remembered the dream, he would have had no trouble guessing whom the pillow represented. He was beginning to understand the meaning of wanting something so bad you can taste it...

"You're still dreaming," he growled at his reflection in the bathroom mirror. "You conveniently forgot it last night, but even proving her innocent won't make her fair game. People have always spent time in her company for the purpose of getting things from her, and now she thinks you did the same to have an alibi. If she's innocent she considers you scum, pal, so you'd better revise those rosy-eyed battle plans."

And stop talking to yourself out loud, he added silently as he bent to the running water. Unless, of course, you can get *her* to do the same thing. Then maybe they'll lock you up in the same padded cell.

Greg tried not to think about anything unofficial while he dressed, but with nothing but Anita's list to occupy his thoughts it didn't work very well. The items Lundgren had brought with him were sparse, and there wasn't a clue among them. The background checks would start becoming available today, the most prominent and therefore most easily-checked people coming through first. Until they did, he could do nothing but poke around.

And hope someone tripped over his feet with some answers. Lundgren had traveled all the way from Europe to take this job, and didn't even get to work it for a single day. Greg had spent some time the night before prowling the shadows, but hadn't seen anyone hurrying through the rain to attend an emergency meeting caused by an unexpected death. Either the people involved in that mess were housed together, or the death wasn't unexpected.

"Which is just plain stupid," Greg muttered with a frown. "Why would an organization bring a man halfway around the world and then kill him? He wasn't carrying anything half a dozen searches could find, so if they wanted him dead, why not do it before he left?"

The answer to that was they would have, so the odds were very much in favor of someone else being responsible for the murder. But who, and for what reason? And what did the organization intend to do to straighten things out? He'd have to check on who made telephone calls last night and this morning. If things didn't go right, calls, reports and new instructions would be made.

Feeling slightly better now that he had one positive course of action, Greg left his room and went down for breakfast. He was only moderately surprised to discover that the Silk Room also served breakfast, but his jeans and white sports shirt weren't acceptable. The Silk Room had a dress code and a reservations list even for that meal, less than formal but much more than casual.

Amused by the thought of people who paid three times the going rate for scrambled eggs and home fries just to have "atmosphere" added, Greg picked up a local newspaper and went to the Cotton Room. He was seated quickly and offered a menu, then was told all about the buffet. That sounded good, so he went and helped himself to some food.

When he got back he found Laine Randall sitting at the next table, sipping coffee and staring at nothing in particular.

"Steady, boy," he told himself silently as he put the plates down on his table. "She must be here for a reason, but maybe we can take advantage of it."

He left his food for a moment, and stepped closer to Laine's table. She was wearing white stretch pants and short white boots that looked to be made of soft leather, and her tunic top matched the green of her eyes. A small, white leather shoulder bag lay on the table near her, and she didn't seem to realize she had company.

"Good morning, Miss Randall," Greg said, fairly certain he was being ignored. "Would you like to join me for breakfast?"

"No thank you," she answered very politely, but her faint smile and distracted gaze weren't aimed at him. He waited for her to add something else, but she didn't.

"If you change your mind, I'm right over here," Greg told her, deliberately giving her the chance to comment on people who pointed out the obvious. When she resisted the bait, he shrugged inwardly and returned to his breakfast.

The food was excellent, but Greg spent quite a lot of his attention on the question of whom Laine would be meeting. He was certain she hadn't just wandered into the restaurant for no reason, but why meet someone *there?* And now that she knew *he* was there, why not move the meeting elsewhere?

Greg finally noticed that his breakfast was gone, but Laine's company hadn't shown up yet. He decided to make another trip to the buffet to see what would happen, but no one signaled the woman while his back was supposedly turned, and she made no effort to leave. He carried his partially refilled plate back and set to work on it, wondering what was going on.

He finished his meal for the second time, but hadn't yet figured out what Laine was up to. Not only was Laine Randall still there and still alone, she hadn't even been checking the time. That suggested she *wasn't* waiting for someone, but the hypothesis wasn't guaranteed. He finished the last of his coffee, signed the check, then got up to leave. He'd see if waiting from a distance brought any answers.

Not far from the restaurant entrance was the beginning of the lobby, so Greg chose a chair and opened the newspaper he hadn't even glanced at yet. He'd be able to keep a casual eye on the restaurant from there, but would be well out of the way.

The paper had a write-up about the murders, but the article was on the bottom of the first page and rather short. Two people had been found dead at the resort, the police suspected murder and were investigating. More news as soon as it's available.

Greg was surprised that so little fuss had been made, and couldn't help wondering why. Had the resort's publicity people paid to have the incident played down? That was likely, but couldn't be the whole answer. They wouldn't have been able to pay off the wire services, or keep information from being released by the sheriff's department. But *had* the story gone to the wire services? Greg would have to check to find out.

And there was something a good deal more obvious than skimpy news coverage. When he put the newspaper down, Laine Randall was sitting on a couch not ten feet away.

Greg blinked at her for a moment, then began to feel annoyed. This time she had no coffee to sip so she was simply sitting there, lost in contemplation. He took a deep, short breath that did nothing to calm the rising anger of suspicion, then got to his feet.

"What do you think you're doing?" he demanded bluntly when he stopped in front of her. "Didn't I tell you not to do any amateur sleuthing?"

"You're blocking my view, Mr. Williams," she said with that same faint smile, making no effort to look up at him. "Please move to one side or the other."

"Your view of what, Miss Randall?" he asked, working not to clench his teeth. "There's nothing here to look at but a wall."

"We're all entitled to our opinions, Mr. Williams. I happen to think there is."

Her faint smile was no longer quite as distant, and that really annoyed him. She was having a grand old time playing the game of follow-your-favorite-suspect. But he couldn't afford to be followed around by anyone, especially Laine Randall.

"Then I'll certainly move out of your way, Miss Randall," he said, shifting to drop down on the couch next to her. "And now that I think about it, you're absolutely right. There *is* something worth looking at here."

Greg wasn't just close to her, he was practically in her lap. Her left arm was pressing into his chest, and when she turned toward him with a sound of protest, he was able to slip his arms around her. An instant later he was tasting lips he'd been dreaming about, but reality was far and away much softer. He held her to him and kissed her a lot more chastely than he would have preferred, but he had to be ready for the explosion.

Which came after a brief hesitation. One instant there was a soft, warm woman in his arms, and the next he was holding a ragingly furious wildcat. Her right hand came up to dig a sharp thumbnail into his left earlobe, and when he pulled back to yelp in pain she stood up and kicked him hard in the left leg.

"You miserable lowlife!" she snarled while he moved fast to get the rest of him out of her reach. "If you ever try that again, I'll..."

Greg watched while she tried to think of something really horrible to promise him. Instead of pursuing the threat, though, she turned and stalked away, her color high, her breathing still furiously uneven. A few people stared after her, then turned to look at him.

"Worth it at twice the price," he murmured, still feeling the ache in his earlobe and the throb in his leg. Holding her had felt incredibly good, and kissing her had made him glad he was wearing jeans. Any more stretch in the material, and he would have needed to be alone for a while to avoid embarrassment. He'd enjoyed kissing Laine, but he'd done it for a more important reason than pleasure. If he ran into trouble Laine Randall would *not* be right behind him, two steps away from getting hurt.

And her current vulnerable position meant it was time for him to get to work. He had to arrange to get the telephone calls checked, and if none of the dossiers had been delivered yet he would wander around the hotel. No one was likely to be sitting around under a sign reading Terrorist Murderer, but you never could tell what else they might do. Rattled people usually got stupid and sloppy.

Someone other than Laine Randall, he amended with a grin as he headed for a telephone. He didn't know how long she would *stay* rattled, but she wasn't likely to come after him again any time soon. If she showed up later he would repeat his act as often as necessary until she gave up.

He chuckled as he reached the small private phone room and closed the door behind him. If she took long enough to give up, by the time the murders were solved they could end up being engaged.

Chapter Eight

Laine slammed the front door of the suite so hard, Bob came out of his room on the run. He stopped short when he saw the expression on her face, and gave her a narrow-eyed frown.

"Okay, what happened?" he demanded, covertly checking her for damage. "That scowl doesn't tell me how many mangled bodies you left behind."

"Only one, and it wasn't mangled nearly well enough," Laine growled in answer, leading the way to the living room. "A little blood would have been nice to see—no, make that a lot of blood. The dirt bag deserves to be entertained on a rack."

"The dirt bag," Bob echoed as he watched her flop down onto a couch. "Since you told me you were going to play rough shadow with Williams, I'll take a wild guess and assume you mean him. What did he do to you?"

"The lowlife kissed me!" she spat, furious all over again. "Right there in the middle of the lobby! And he thought it was funny!"

"It is," Bob said with a sudden grin, all signs of worry gone. "The bad guys on your series pull guns or knives, but this one kissed you. Considering your looks, a true-to-life episode would have had it happening a long time ago."

"You're as funny as he is," Laine muttered, turning away from his amusement. She knew she was bothered about something other than a simple kiss, and she didn't have to wonder what it was. He'd taken her by surprise when he'd put his arms around her, and she had to admit she was attracted to the man who was her primary suspect.

Laine blew out a sharp breath of self-disgust, then lay back on the couch. All through dinner the evening before, she'd caught herself wondering what it would be like to be held by that mystery man. He was built so strongly, with real muscle. And those stubborn lips that smiled with so much charm—what would it feel like to kiss them?

Well, now she knew, and the experience had been more pleasant than she had expected. The kiss he'd stolen had been very gentle, teasing rather than intrusive, playful rather than demanding. A man like that had no business being playful, and he certainly had no right to tease her. She would have to show him the kiss had meant nothing to her.

"I'm going to make him sorry he did that," she promised aloud, then turned her head to look at Bob. "How did your calls go?"

"As smooth as if it had been written in a script," he answered from the chair he'd taken. "Lieutenant Halloran was only too glad to help, and Sheriff Stoddard was duly impressed. When Halloran hung up, I told the sheriff what you wanted and which part of the investigation you'd decided to cover. Instead of laughing or hanging up on me, he hesitated very briefly then said to go ahead. But I wasn't to let you do your snooping alone.''

''Which means he really is afraid there's a werewolf involved,'' Laine said, sitting up slowly to look bleakly at Bob. ''If that's true, I wonder how enthusiastically he's pursuing the other possibilities in the investigation. Is he trying hard to disprove old wives' tales, or just going through the motions because he knows the *real* truth?''

''We should find out when we get the file he's sending,'' Bob replied with a shrug, but not a disinterested one. ''If I were in his place, I'd follow the faintest, least possible trail to keep from having to admit the perp is very likely a guy with real heavy five o'clock shadow.''

''I agree,'' Laine said after considering the point very briefly, then she got to her feet. ''In any event, there's only one way to find out. I'm going to call the sheriff, and tell him about someone who has aroused my suspicions. He isn't involved in *my* part of the investigation, so the sheriff and his men really ought to handle the matter. Stoddard might be so glad to find something normal to check, he'll move on it immediately.''

''Why are *my* suspicions suddenly aroused?'' Bob asked, once again staring at her narrowly. ''What did your kissing bandit do that caught your attention?''

''Well, for one thing he was out in the rain last night, *after* the murders,'' Laine said, counting on her fingers. ''For a second, he tried to deny knowing the male victim, and in that he was lying. For a third, he has no legitimate business here, since he's not really on vacation. For a fourth—well, I'll find a fourth if it's needed. The first three should be enough to justify taking him someplace official for more than casual questioning. Maybe a fingerprint check will supply some much-needed answers.''

"I can see he really got to you with that kiss," Bob observed quietly, leaning back in his chair. "Are you absolutely sure you want to turn him over to the police? You might get a result you're not expecting."

"Like what?" Laine asked, letting brashness cover the real hesitancy she felt. She didn't *want* to turn the mystery man over to the police, but she owed it to Nissa's memory not to leave any possibility unconsidered. Besides, chances were they would just question him a little, then let him go. For some unexplainable reason she would have bet money that he had no police record, and the experience would simply serve to teach him not to start up with her again.

"Well, what if they find nothing on him, and have to release him with an apology?" Bob answered. "Do you think for one minute he won't *know* who he has to thank for being picked up? What if he gets back here and comes looking for you?"

Laine said something reassuring and laughed off Bob's concern, but most of her wasn't paying attention to the performance. In her mind, she was picturing a furious Greg Williams coming after her. The image made her want to swallow hard, but then she straightened her shoulders. She'd told him she wasn't afraid of him, and that was the truth. Wasn't it?

With that bolstering thought she walked over to the telephone, ignoring whatever small qualms she still felt. She really could take care of herself, and with Bob around, what did she have to worry about?

"THIS IS RIDICULOUS," Greg stated to the deputy sitting down opposite him in the very modern but equally featureless interrogation room. "Do you know how long you've kept me sitting here?"

"Somethin' came up that had to be taken care of," the deputy responded with a calm, amused smile. He was a tall, brown-haired man, easygoing and with only a slight accent, the sort who never let anything impress him very much. "I do appreciate your waitin', though."

"What choice did I have?" Greg countered with a glance at the second deputy who had stayed in the room with him. That one was the size of a monster, and hadn't said a word. "Would you like to tell me now why I was brought here? I haven't been put under arrest, but I also haven't been allowed to leave."

"We asked for a set of your fingerprints, but you refused to give them," the deputy observed as he looked through some papers, ignoring Greg's question. "Would you like to tell me why you did that, Mr. Williams?"

"You're not entitled to my fingerprints unless you arrest me," Greg told the man with a calm of his own. "I also have to be informed of the charges, and allowed to call a lawyer. What is it I'm suspected of doing, Deputy?"

"Last night, when you heard people had been killed, you went runnin' out to get a look at 'em," the deputy said, finally raising a brown-eyed stare to his face. "When you were questioned you said you thought they might not be dead, and you went out to help if you could. Are you a doctor, Mr. Williams?"

"At a time like that you don't stop to think about what you know, you just run to help," Greg answered sourly.

"Like any other Good Samaritan would have done," the deputy agreed with a nod. "And when you got there, did you recognize the dead man, Mr. Williams?"

"It was dark and raining, and he was covered with blood," Greg replied with a shrug. "I thought he looked familiar, but I wasn't certain until I was told who he was."

"Even though you traveled all the way from New York with him?" the deputy asked. "It seems you were on the same plane with him, the same train, and even got to the resort in the same van. When did you first decide to visit that resort, Mr. Williams?"

"When one of my business associates told me I was going," Greg returned very flatly. "If you want more details about that, you'll have to charge me and let me call a lawyer. Are you ready to do that?"

The deputy made a noncommittal noise and looked down at his papers again, giving Greg a minute to breathe. If he'd been instructed to tell the local police who he was and why he was there, it would already have been done. Any leak at all could reach the wrong ears and ruin his chances of finding out what he needed to know, so he would bluff his way through as long as possible. But if they decided to charge him . . .

"So you're not really here on vacation, and you knew the dead man better than you're letting on," the deputy summed up, then looked at him again. "Is any of that the reason you took a second walk in the rain last night, after all the excitement was over? Or were you worryin' about helpin' somebody, and didn't stop to think?''

''How did you know I—'' Greg began, and then it hit him. ''Laine Randall! *She's* the one who put you up to this! Don't you realize she's as much of a suspect as I am, and maybe even more? She didn't just *happen* to know one of the victims, she came here with her. Why didn't you drag *her* down here?''

''Miss Randall says you broke into her suite last night and threatened her,'' the deputy stated, now ignoring Greg's anger. ''Is that the sort of thing Good Samaritans do where you come from?''

''I didn't break into her suite, I walked in through the unlocked patio door,'' Greg corrected. ''I went there to see if she was all right, and I didn't threaten her. When she said something about getting involved with investigating the murders, I warned her not to stick an amateur nose into official police business.''

''That I have to agree with,'' the deputy said with a nod. ''But why did you think it was your business to warn her off? The fact that you didn't want her pointing any fingers at *you?* Everything she's said so far has held up.''

''Wait a minute,'' Greg said, frowning thoughtfully at the man. ''Why are you backing her up? You've found out something about her, something that takes her off the suspect list. Tell me what it is.''

''Mr. Williams, you seem to be havin' trouble understandin' that you're here to *answer* questions, not ask them,'' the deputy countered with a sigh. ''We've got two people lyin' dead in the morgue, and we mean to know who put them there. We're goin' to keep goin' over this till I get answers I like, even if it takes all day and most of the night.''

"Sorry, Deputy, but you won't like the answers I have," Greg said with a grin. His instincts had been right, and Laine Randall *was* innocent.

"Look, Mr. Williams—" the deputy began, but Greg had had enough of defense. Now he was going on the offense.

"No, you look, Deputy," he interrupted. "If Miss Randall was all that frightened by my supposed break-in last night, why did she wait until today to report it? And if her accusations are all that accurate, why didn't I do something about them last night, when she accused me to my face?"

"Didn't you?" the deputy asked, but now there was a shadow of doubt in his eyes. "You threatened the woman—"

"I told her what could happen if she crowded a murderer too hard," he interrupted again. "I'm not free to talk about the business that brought me here, so she immediately assumed I was guilty of involvement. When she said so I realized she was snooping, and tried to get her to back off for her own good. As it turned out, I didn't succeed."

"What do you mean?" the deputy asked, narrowing his eyes. "If you're talkin' about bein' brought down here—"

"I'm talking about the way she followed me around this morning," Greg cut in. "She knew she couldn't keep me from seeing her, so she went the opposite route. Every time I looked up, there she was, stepping on my shadow. I'm her favorite suspect, and she wanted me to know it."

The deputy's expression flickered, and Greg grinned.

"She didn't mention that, did she?" he guessed aloud. "And I'll bet she also didn't mention what I did to get rid of her. It should tell you why we're here now, wasting each other's time."

"All right, tell me," the deputy conceded, knowing Greg was waiting for some sign of interest.

"I took her in my arms and kissed her," Greg said, enjoying the new look on the deputy's face. "There were a number of witnesses, so you needn't take my word for it. She blew up and half beat me to death, then stormed out of the lobby. I'll bet anything that her call to you came *after* that incident."

"I'll talk to the sheriff about that," the man muttered, gathering his papers together before standing. "It could make a difference." He walked to the door, paused to look back at Greg, muttered, "Kissed her," then left shaking his head. The deputy finally seemed impressed, and that was amusing.

Greg settled back in the very uncomfortable wooden chair, thinking about the incident himself. Laine had obviously been so furious she'd decided to use the police to get even, and that was something Greg would be talking to her about. She could have screwed things up for him very badly, and all because he hadn't let her play detective. The very least she deserved was a good talking to.

He sat up straight as a new thought occurred to him. If she was all that determined to play detective, why would she have her favorite suspect picked up by the police? That would leave her no one to pester—unless she'd decided to branch out. There were a lot of other people at the resort, all of whom would provide limitless opportunities for poking and snooping.

"I have to get out of here," Greg said to the deputy as he rose to his feet.

"I can't authorize your leaving," the man answered mildly in a rich, cultured voice, making no effort to move from where he stood. "You'll have to wait for the sheriff."

Greg wanted to make a nasty comment, but it would have been useless for anything but causing trouble. He needed to get out of there to keep Laine Randall from putting her beautiful but unbelievably stubborn neck on the block. He sat back down, prepared to wait no more than a few short minutes. Just as he'd decided he'd waited long enough, the other deputy came back in.

"It's about time," Greg said, immediately getting to his feet. "I'll need a ride back to the hotel."

"And I'm sure you'll get it as soon as we're done with you, Mr. Williams," the man said, sitting again in his own chair. "The computer says that Gregory Williams, at the address given on your identification, doesn't exist. Would you like to explain where the silly thing made its mistake? Don't tell me you kissed *it*, too?"

Greg groaned and slumped back in the chair, feeling the urge to kill. His ID was supposed to be fully backgrounded, but in the rush to get him into position someone had obviously forgotten to do the proper paperwork. If he hadn't been picked up the omission might never have been noticed, but now he had *that* to explain without giving anything away.

And he had to do it fast enough to get back to Laine before *she* did something dangerously stupid. He'd really have to thank her for getting him involved with the police—if she was still alive.

Chapter Nine

"...and so it became obvious where my duty lay," Laine told the crowd around her, smiling into their admiring faces.

"And your duty lay in helping the police," a dewy-eyed woman said, her expression one of reverence. "Oh, Miss Randall, you're the most marvelous person I've ever seen. Donating *your* time as an experienced detective, just to help out these backwoods officials. I hope they're grateful to you."

"They're absolutely delighted, of course," Laine assured the woman—and everyone else—with a self-satisfied smirk. "But they'll be even more delighted when I catch the criminal for them."

"But without a script, how do you expect to do that?" an amused male voice asked. "Doesn't all your vast experience come from a film set?"

The man speaking was in the second row of the crowd, but he wasn't hidden by any means. They all stood in the giant pool area, and he was dressed—or undressed—for the occasion. Over six feet tall, brown hair with smoky gray eyes, a body that had every woman in sight licking her lips. Laine felt like laughing in his face, but only her prepared response showed.

"The key words to remember are 'vast experience,'" she told the man with cool, regal amusement. "What's the difference *how* you get the experience, as long as you have it?"

"That's a point of some sort," he allowed with a grin that made him even more handsome, then raised the glass he held to her. "Whatever, I wish you good luck."

"Thank you," Laine answered automatically, already having dismissed him in her mind. "Now, I want you all to understand what I'm doing, so you'll be able to help me as much as possible. Someone got the idea that a *werewolf* committed the murders, and that's the part I'm investigating. I'll talk to you all one at a time, and while you're waiting your turn I want you to think back. Did anyone behave oddly yesterday? Look rattled this morning? Fail to show up somewhere last night? *Anything* that struck you as strange, I want to know about. I'll be with you as soon as I freshen my drink."

She smiled around again and then left them to their startled exclamations, heading directly toward one of the pool bars.

"Another Virgin Mary," she told the barkeep, sitting on a stool in an effort to unwind. She'd been at it for hours, starting after lunch. The resort's guests were spread out doing different things, and that meant she had to go wherever they were, and interview everyone willing to be interviewed.

Bob had given up hanging around a couple of hours earlier, realizing she was safe among so many people. He would be back with her again that night, when they visited the Show Room and main casino, but for now he'd taken the coward's way out.

Which was what Laine almost wished *she* could do. She'd spent what felt like forever listening to the most ridiculous stories, none of which were any help at all. Everyone laughed at the idea of a werewolf, but beneath the laughter was a small note of fearful belief. They'd all seen the movies as children just as she had, and because of that they couldn't scoff with as much sincerity as they would have liked.

"There you go, ma'am," the bartender said, smiling as he handed her a fresh drink. She signed the tab he also handed her, showing her suite key at the same time. After this group she would go back to her suite, take a shower and a nap, then dress for dinner and the night ahead. Maybe tonight she would get a lead...

"I think my brother was a werewolf," a voice at her left shoulder said. "He spent most of his time shaving, especially when the moon was full. But he doesn't happen to be here right now, so I suppose the story doesn't help."

Laine looked up to see the heckler from the crowd, his grin half amused and half ridiculing.

"You can laugh if you like, but this happens to be a serious matter," she told him with just the right amount of stiffness, taking her drink and standing. "I appreciate you telling me you didn't see anything, but now I have others to question."

"I didn't say I didn't see anything," he disagreed, moving himself smoothly into her way. "What I'm seeing right now is certainly worth looking at, and I might have seen something last night without realizing it. Let's discuss the possibility over dinner."

"I'll be much too busy considering what I've already learned," she told him with a professional smile. The look in his eyes was tiringly familiar, and she wasn't in the mood to be patient. "Would you like to step out of my way, or don't you mind the idea of wearing a glass of tomato juice?"

"I'm not giving up," he said with a smile to match hers, slowly moving to one side. "The only reason you're spending time on nonsense is because you don't have any *one* to spend it on. I intend to change that, starting tonight. Instead of asking about werewolves, you'll be asking about Jeremy Roberts."

"Jeremy Roberts?" Laine repeated, deliberately giving him a vague look. Then she smiled radiantly. "Never heard of him."

And that was without doubt an exit line. As she strode away Laine wondered if she was supposed to have missed the flash of anger in Jeremy's eyes. He hadn't liked being dismissed, but that was too bad. He was lucky she hadn't told him to find a professional to write his lines. The ones he had were definitely of the amateur variety.

Most of the people in the pool area were eager to discuss the possibility of werewolves, but as time dragged on Laine had to admit she was getting nowhere. Not only hadn't anyone seen anything, no one was even interested in leaving. The idea of werewolves was exciting in its frightfulness, and most of the guests were looking forward to what would happen next.

Laine stuck it out to the bitter end, then left the pool area by the outside walkway. The relief over being able to escape was incredible, especially since so many people had left before her. The late afternoon shadows were lengthening, and most of the guests had headed back to their accommodations to rest up for that night's festivities.

"And for the second appearance of the werewolf," Laine muttered to herself in disgust as she walked toward the main stretch that would take her to her suite. "What turns nice, ordinary people into such ghouls?"

Maybe they're *not* being ghoulish, another side of her argued silently. A murder like that seems unreal, and unless you've personally lost someone to the crime, it must seem more like entertainment than reality. It was so outrageous, the police would never have had the point investigated. Someone with a badge and official standing would feel like a fool asking about—

Laine stopped short, but the sound she thought she'd heard wasn't repeated. There was a tall privacy hedge to her left, and a stretch of blank hotel wall ahead to her right. Lush bushes stood in the shadows beside the wall in an attempt to make up for the lack of windows, but that's all that was there. The walkway both ahead and behind her was empty. She was totally alone, completely cut off from everyone else in the hotel. Except for that odd noise...

"It must have been the wind," Laine told herself, shifting her shoulder bag higher. "Or, since it's dead calm and hot, your imagination. Let's save that for a better time, shall we?"

Such a sensible idea had to be accepted at once, so she began walking again. It came to her that she'd forgotten to ask Bob what he'd found out about the full moon, but the question would have to wait. So what if the moon sometimes came out when it was still daylight? The back doors leading into the hotel weren't all *that* far ahead...

And that was when the husky figure stepped quickly out of the bushes into her path. He wore old, faded jeans and a plaid shirt that had seen better days, and the features of his face were distorted by a stocking mask,. Laine's heart lurched as she stopped short, but before she could take a step back to give herself more room, she heard something behind her.

A glance back showed a second man, dressed the same way including the mask, blocking her retreat. Panic gripped her insides the way it had only once before in her life, but she knew better than to let it show.

"If you boys are looking for autographs, you'll have to come back later," she said, moving slowly to her left to get both of them in view. "That last group at the pool gave me writer's cramp."

It was possible the one to her left smiled, but the stocking mask made it difficult to tell. What frightened her most was the fact that they weren't saying anything, not a demand for her money or a warning to mind her own business. They didn't have to be there because of the questions she'd been asking, but any other reason would be too incredible a coincidence.

And she didn't know what their intentions were. Very slowly and deliberately she took her shoulder bag and tossed it behind her to the right, but the two pairs of eyes staring at her paid no attention to it. So much for a robbery theory.

Laine had faced stunt men for on-camera attack scenes, but those had always been very carefully rehearsed. A fight was more closely choreographed than a dance; one wrong move on the part of an actor or stunt person, and someone was likely to get seriously hurt. She had taught herself to pay attention to nothing but what was coming at her, and to respond to nothing but properly cued moves.

Now the man to her left made a wordless sound, but the one on the right had already begun moving toward her. She ignored the sound as her hands came up into fists, her feet already positioned with her weight evenly distributed between them. Her heart was pounding like crazy. The shot of adrenaline brought on by her fear would add to her strength and speed, giving her the help she was very much afraid she would need.

The thug to her right continued to come at her in an almost leisurely way, totally ignoring the way she stood. She was an actress, after all, and had to be good at pretending. His attitude was so apparent, Laine could almost hear the rationalizing words echoing in his head.

But she wasn't pretending.. As his right hand reached for her she twisted her left shoulder back and away, at the same time bringing her right leg up and out in a side kick aimed at his knee.

The man screamed and fell backward to the ground clutching his leg, but Laine had already shifted her stance to the left. The second man was coming toward her, and the fact that his friend was down didn't mean she was halfway done.

Her second opponent had gone into a casual unarmed defense stance. His knees were bent and his fists were up, but he didn't look as if he were really ready to fight like that. He threw a fist that she was able to avoid, and it came from shoulder rather than belt level.

Laine aimed a front kick at his knee, but the man blocked it. His forearm came down hard on her shin before she could connect, and then he was dancing away. He came in again to throw a kick at her, and

Laine's block, although effective, didn't have his strength.

Which encouraged him to come at her again, this time with both a kick and a punch. Laine blocked the kick and ducked the punch, but the man's clumsiness was affecting *her* balance. She stumbled a little trying to put more distance between them, letting his size force her into retreating rather than attacking. She realized immediately that she'd made a mistake, but it was already too late. He was coming right after her, and if she backed away again she would trip over the attacker on the ground.

Her pursuer's arms were coming up to pull her to him, and Laine realized he was close enough to do just that. She aimed a blow to his heart region and let it go, but his arm swept down to partially block it, then up again to grab at her. He'd grunted in pain from the deflected blow, and his very low cursing showed how angry he was. When he got his hands on her, *she* would be the one in pain.

And then he was suddenly gone from in front of her, pulled away to face another opponent who was even angrier than he. The newcomer reached back, then hurled a large, square fist into the masked face. Laine's former attacker staggered, all but out on his feet, and then the side kick slammed into his middle. With that much strength behind it, the blow didn't simply knock him down. He all but flew past the place where his friend with the broken leg was trying to crawl away from, and sprawled unmoving on the ground.

"Laine, are you all right?" the newcomer demanded, coming close fast to put his arms around her. "You're trembling. Did he hurt you?"

It actually took Laine a moment to realize that it wasn't Bob who had saved her. It was Greg Williams who stood there holding her to him, just as if he had a right to do that. There were also a number of security people running up. First there's nobody, and then everyone arrives at once.

"Of course I'm trembling," she managed to say in a steady voice as she pushed away from the warmth of Greg's big body. "Do you always appear out of thin air?"

"It so happens I was looking for you," he answered, his frowning inspection of her still not quite satisfied. "I was walking to your suite, and happened to see you down here. I shouted for security, then came ahead to ask for the next dance. Are you sure you're all right?"

"I'd be a hell of a lot better if I had another hundred pounds of muscle, like some people I could mention," she muttered, turning to look again at the still unconscious second attacker. Two of the security men had stripped the masks from both of the thugs, and a third stood talking into a hand radio. "If *I'd* done that, I'd probably be throwing a celebration party right now."

"You did half of it, which surprises and pleases me," he said, the words sounding amused. "Next time I'll know I can walk to your rescue instead of having to run. I may be getting a little too old for this."

Considering the fact that he hadn't even been breathing hard at any time, Laine considered the comment ludicrous. She ran a hand through her hair, feeling the weakness in her knees, then resolutely headed for where her shoulder bag lay.

"I'd be curious to know why those two came to dance with you," Greg said, following her. "Couldn't they wait until the music started tonight?"

"They didn't say," Laine told him, smiling faintly to herself at the memory. "Why don't you ask them?"

"Good idea," he responded immediately. "At least *you* were smart enough to leave yours conscious."

He walked over to the attacker on the ground while Laine bent to retrieve her shoulder bag, and she could hear him putting the question to the man with the broken knee. Greg's voice was hard and commanding, but the only response he got was a string of four-letter words.

"It looks like we'll have to let the sheriff do the asking," Greg said, light eyes still showing annoyance. "Come on, I'll walk you home. The authorities will know where to find you when they want you."

Laine let him take her arm and start them both walking, trying to figure out how to say what she had to. The words weren't much of a problem, but she wasn't sure she could control her tone. Professional or not, some things were too personal to treat like just another script. At the very least she had to try.

"It looks like I have to thank you for saving me," she said, working very hard to keep the words neutral. "If you hadn't come along, that second attacker would have got me."

"Not necessarily," he disagreed, and Laine could feel the way he looked down at her. "You're not afraid to hurt your opponent, and that's all to the good. You probably could have done him a lot of damage. But you don't *have* to thank me."

"Of course I do," Laine began in protest, but he didn't let her finish.

"No, you *don't,*" he insisted, the words very flat and final. "'Have to' means you feel you're being forced into it, and I'd rather have no thanks at all than forced ones. Do you think you might forget my unreliable true character for the moment, and sound like you mean what you say? Or would you rather forget the whole thing?"

"How am I supposed to forget that my closest friend has been murdered?" she demanded, stopping short to stare up into blue eyes that seemed to be trying hard not to show hurt. "Do I shrug it off as one of life's little twists of rotten luck? After all, a man as handsome as you couldn't *possibly* be guilty of involvement. How do I know you didn't *stage* that little attack, just so you could come riding to the rescue? Life would be a lot simpler for you if I became convinced of your innocence."

"I can't possibly picture you being that cooperative," he told her sourly, his expression matching. "Just for the record, I had nothing to do with that attack except for the part you saw. On the other hand, though, it might be a good idea to keep in mind for the future. The attack part, I mean. I think you can find your own way home from here."

They were standing near the doors leading into the main building, and he simply walked away and disappeared through them. Laine stared after him for a moment, then turned and headed for her suite. When she closed the door and entered the living room, Bob came out of his bedroom and joined her.

"Laine, is anything wrong? You look—odd."

"I feel odd," she answered, pouring herself a drink at the bar.

Bob refused to let her tell the story until she was sitting down, but then he listened in grim silence. The fury in his eyes was very difficult to watch, so Laine looked away until she'd told it all.

"And all that time I sat here with my feet up, comfortably reading," he growled when she was through. "Well, you can be damned sure *that* won't happen again. Lucky for me your favorite suspect was hanging around. I'll have to thank him for being there when I should have been."

"Then you'd better get the manual on how to thank him properly," Laine said, finishing the last of her drink. "When I didn't do it right, he threw it back at me."

"All right, what did you say?" Bob asked in that tone of controlled patience he used so often. "I know you, Laine, and if you're being really sarcastic you're feeling especially guilty. The man jumped in and kept you from getting killed, and what did you say to thank him?"

"Why does it have to be *my* fault?" she flared, getting to her feet and heading back to the bar. "Can't it just as easily be his?"

The silence grew thick behind her back as she refilled her glass. Laine sipped at her freshened drink, hating the quiet, then found herself blurting out the conversation she'd had with Greg Williams. The silence continued a moment beyond the end of her admission, and then Bob's hand touched her shoulder.

"You believe him," Bob stated, his voice gentle. "You may not want to, but you still do. Would it help to know that I believe him, too?"

"I didn't know you were partial to blonds," Laine said, moving away from his hand. "Does Ann know?"

"Laine, you're fighting your own instincts," Bob came back in exasperation. "It has to have occurred to you that if *he* staged the attack, the two men would hardly be in custody now. He would *not* have alerted hotel security before charging in, and would have found a good reason to leave the two creeps unguarded after his win. Don't you think so?"

"I suppose," Laine grudged, aware that Bob hadn't asked a question. "I also suppose that's why I tried to thank him, but he wasn't having any."

"I don't blame him," Bob said immediately. "You've been accusing him almost nonstop, and can't even manage a simple thank-you without grudging the words. I'd say you ought to be ashamed—if I didn't know you already were."

"I'm not ashamed," she muttered in return, but they both knew she was lying. The man had *saved* her, and she had thanked him by suggesting he was responsible for the attack. "But why couldn't I tell *him* I believed him?"

"Because he's guilty of being too handsome," Bob told her. "You've had so many bad experiences with good-looking men, you flinch by reflex."

"I suppose you're right," Laine responded obligingly, then turned to look at Bob. "Are you sure you're not studying to be a shrink? No, don't answer that, I don't want to know. I am *not* prejudiced against handsome men, I simply don't trust them. And for very good reasons, in case you've forgotten. They've been guilty up till now, so why should Greg Williams be any different?"

"Because they weren't guilty of murder," Bob pronounced, staring at her to emphasize the point. "I'm not saying he isn't involved, Laine. I don't know enough to decide either way, but neither do you."

Laine knew he was right, but she was too bothered to want to admit it. Instead she sighed, then rapidly changed the subject.

"You said you were reading," she remembered aloud. "Were you by any chance reading the case file sent over by the sheriff?"

"No, I finished *that* not long after it got here," he answered. "There isn't much to it, and what there is isn't pleasant. Do you want to see it now?"

"As soon as I've had a shower," she decided with another sigh. "I'm all knotted up and need to relax for tonight."

"Speaking about nights, I've got your information on the full moon. It should interest you to know that *tonight* is the actual full moon, but many people consider the night before and the night after as part of the event. If you look at it that way, full moon is last night, tonight and tomorrow night."

"Great," Laine responded. "Now see if you can find out what time the moon rises. No sense in skulking around in the bushes wasting hours, not if the werewolf's appointment schedule has him booked elsewhere for the time."

"Come on, Laine, you're not serious." Bob's suddenly worried voice followed her toward her bedroom. "We're not going out *looking* for that thing? In the dark? Without even a silver tea service? Laine, please say you're joking."

The plaintive note in his voice made her chuckle, but she went into her bedroom without answering. He'd get used to the idea, and it wasn't as if he were afraid for himself, after all. When they went prowling that night, she would be prepared.

"But how prepared will I be if I happen to meet Greg Williams again?" she asked herself, putting her glass aside while she took off her clothes. She knew she owed him an apology, but she wasn't sure she could do it without starting another fight. He'd definitely saved her from something he *hadn't* arranged, but that didn't change the fact that he was still a mystery man.

And a mystery man who had gotten the sheriff to let him go. Laine had almost forgotten about that, and the fact that Greg Williams had been free to save her could turn out to be significant. If she did meet him again, there were a couple of questions she would have to ask....

Chapter Ten

Greg Williams went straight to his room, anger making him see red as he walked past Anita without more than a nod in her direction. A moment later she was in the doorway watching him splash water on his face in the bathroom.

"What's going on?" she asked. "And what have you done to your hand?"

"First off, I spent the day at the sheriff's office, sitting in an interrogation room answering questions," he told her, a growl clear in his voice. "When I finally broke loose I went looking for Miss Randall, to thank her for convincing the sheriff I deserved special attention. I found her in the middle of being attacked, so I stepped in and quieted things down. Now I'm here, and I'd like to know if you have anything worth reporting."

"Nothing like what you do," she answered, her reflection showing raised brows. "How did Laine Randall manage to talk the sheriff into picking you up? He's an experienced cop from Chicago, much too levelheaded to be affected by a smile and a wiggle."

"How she convinced him could be important," Greg answered, turning the water off and reaching for a towel. "I agree that smiles would never do it, so let's look for the real reason. And I have a bone to pick with Control. My background as Greg Williams was conspicuously absent from all computer files."

Anita made a very unladylike comment, then shook her head. "But if your background came up a blank, how did you get them to let you go? Don't tell me you broke jail, and now you're a wanted man?"

"I had a short, private talk with the sheriff," Greg told her, knowing how annoyed he looked. "They'd been trying to get me to donate a set of fingerprints, but as soon as the question came up I realized they already had partials. I opened the door of the car they picked me up in, at the time noticing only in passing that the outside door handle looked polished. When we left the car, it was through the other door. I gave the sheriff a clear thumbprint in exchange for the partials, then told him what file to look in."

"The emergency file," Anita said with a nod of relief. "It supplies a picture ID without name or affiliation, and states that full records are restricted. Was that enough for him?"

"For the moment." Greg matched her nod. "He wants to know what's going on, and if I don't have some hard answers for him soon, I'll be back in that interrogation room. I'm sure he's also sending queries to every government agency he can think of, which means he'll eventually have some answers whether I give them to him or not."

"Then we'll have to move as fast as we can, before word leaks out," Anita said, now looking thoughtful. "You've had a lot of reading matter delivered, but before you get to it I still have a few questions. How does an attack on Laine Randall fit into this, and since when do you get so flurried you scrape your knuckles delivering a hand blow?''

Greg tried to maintain his anger, but she had him pegged and there was no sense in trying to deny it.

"Okay, okay, so I lost it for a minute," he admitted, tossing the towel aside. "Even at a dead run, it took me too long to reach the scene of action. That slime was almost my size, and he was so intent on getting his hands on Laine that he didn't even hear me coming. She was doing better than most defending herself, but I could see he meant to do her real harm. I was so angry that when I pulled him off her I put a fist in his face. It may hurt more than a soft tissue target, but there's also a lot more satisfaction."

"If you say so," she returned with a smile. "But all of that still leaves us with the question of why anyone would *want* to hurt her. Could she have been staging a publicity stunt, or be trying to prove how innocent she is?"

"I thought of that, but it doesn't fit," Greg told her, leading the way back into the sitting room area. "If something about Laine Randall made the sheriff cooperate with her, she doesn't *need* a phony attack to better her position. And if it *was* phony, she wouldn't have broken the leg of one of the attackers. She would have arranged to be jumped in front of witnesses, and the mystery attackers would have gotten away."

"It looks like your dream girl may be innocent after all," Anita said, taking a chair while he poured himself some soda water from the bar. "If the attack was real, it could have happened because she learned something during all that questioning she did."

"I knew it!" Greg growled, slamming the bottle of soda water back into place. "She threw me to the dogs because she didn't want me interfering with her own private investigation! I ought to—who was she questioning, and what about?"

"She was questioning everybody who would talk to her, and you don't want to *know* what about," Anita replied, then flinched at the look he gave her. "All right, all right, so you do want to know. She's apparently investigating a minor theory going around about who the murderer is. Or what he is. A werewolf."

"A what?" Greg asked, feeling as though he'd run full speed into a brick wall. "Anita, you may have missed the point, but I'm not in the mood for jokes. There's no such thing as a werewolf."

"That's not what a large number of deputies and Laine Randall think," Anita disagreed. "It seems there were clues at the murder scene pointing to the possibility, so she's looking for a werewolf. She's grandstanding a lot while she's doing it, but she seems to be completely serious."

"If Randall is chasing ghoulies and ghosties, why would anyone have her attacked? The murderer should be encouraging her after busting a gut laughing."

"As I see it, there are three possibilities," Anita told him, crossing her legs as she got more comfortable in the chair. "One, Laine Randall was told something she shouldn't have been told, something that points directly to the real murderer. Two, someone wants everyone to believe she's getting close to the truth. In other words, that it *was* a werewolf who did it."

"That's an excellent idea," Greg said thoughtfully, sitting down opposite Anita. "Encourage everyone to go baying up the wrong trail while you sit back and laugh. The attack was supposed to discourage her from doing what they don't want her to stop doing. What's the third possibility?''

"That it really was a werewolf, and they really do want to stop her from finding out," Anita said, then held up a hand. "And don't look at me that way. It may not be a realistic possibility, but it still has to be considered. Don't forget there's actual evidence to back up the theory."

"I wish there was some way to get a look at the police file," Greg said, even more unhappy than he had been. "I'd planned on ghosting into headquarters for an after midnight tour, but after today that's out. If Stoddard doesn't have me covered, he's not half the cop I think he is. I'm sure he's expecting me to lead him where he wants to go, not realizing I'm stumbling around trying to pry a blindfold off."

"Why don't you have your girlfriend ask to see the file," Anita suggested, the phoniest innocent look on her face that Greg had ever seen. "After all, now that you're her hero you can ask for anything you like."

"She's not my girlfriend, and I'm not her hero," Greg answered, staring at the drink he hadn't yet tasted. "She all but thanked me through gritted teeth, then got around to mentioning she thought it possible that *I* was the one who arranged the attack. Let's just say we parted on a less than friendly note."

"Greg, she's grieving for a very close friend," Anita told him gently, no longer teasing. "She's also out for the blood of the one who did it. If she *wasn't* suspicious of you she'd be a twit, and the record shows you don't like idiots. Even if they happen to be spectacularly beautiful. Since you've come to a full stop, give it a chance. At least you can be fairly certain *she's* innocent."

"That's right, I can," he agreed with surprise, wondering why he hadn't thought of that. It probably had to do with the fact that Laine was driving him crazy, past the point of rational thought.

"If you're going to sit there fantasizing, I'm going back to the staff area to find some fun of my own." Anita's words brought him back to the real world with a crash. "Since I'm now off duty I intended helping you read all that background info you were sent, but if you think I'm going to plow through it alone..."

"Okay, I surrender," he conceded with a laugh, holding up his free hand. "It's past time to get some work done, especially if I want to clear my good name. And if I want to keep Laine Randall's name from becoming Mud. If she's talking to the wrong people, I can drag her away from them only if I know who they are."

"And let's not forget to check if any of them have ever been accused of being a werewolf," Anita said, getting up to go toward the large package sitting discreetly on a side table. "We'd look awfully foolish if there was something there and we ignored it."

"I was about to suggest you get a disposable cup, and I would pour you a drink," Greg said, getting up to follow her. "Now I can see for sure that you don't need it. Do you really think anyone would put something like that into a background file? You might as well look for what they wore on Halloween, or what they do on Friday the 13th."

"I suppose you're right," Anita allowed with a sigh, turning to look at him. "But what happens if we *do* end up with a werewolf as the murderer? Do we avoid the laughter by never mentioning it in our report?"

"We keep from mentioning it to avoid the men in the white jackets," Greg corrected. "First they'd laugh, and then they'd have us locked up. Laine Randall can get away with talking about it because people *expect* actresses to be eccentric. People like you and me are supposed to be normal."

"Now there's a laugh," Anita said with a grin. "If we were normal, would we be spending our time at a fancy resort sitting in a room reading files?"

"Maybe not, but I wonder if it's what the average murderer is doing," Greg said, frowning at the sudden thought. "Would the people we're after have paper files on the ones they mean to contact and deal with? And what in hell will they be dealing *for?*"

"That's something we still have to find out," Anita said. "Do you think it's possible that's what Laine Randall accidently learned?"

"That's what I mean to look into tonight," Greg said, reaching for the package of data. "And Laine Randall *will* answer my questions, or I'll know the reason why."

Seeing the look in his light eyes, Anita refrained from commenting. He was worried about his dream girl, so he intended to be firm with her for her own good. She couldn't wait to see the fireworks explode.

Chapter Eleven

"...so that's it, ma'am," the deputy said, shifting his hat around and around by the brim with both hands. "Those two 'r just a couple a street toughs, an' if they were paid in cash like they claim, they don't *hafta* know who hired 'em. They had the money an' their orders, so they did the job. Or tried to."

"And their orders were to hurt Miss Randall, but not seriously," Bob said, his tone sounding controlled to Laine. "We appreciate knowing that, Deputy, and from now on I'll be with her at all times. Please thank the sheriff for us."

"Yes, sir," the deputy said. "You bein' with her oughta do it. I guess I'll be goin' now."

Even with Bob herding him toward the door, it took more than usual effort to be rid of the man. Laine found his attraction to her vaguely amusing, but she was too busy thinking about the information she'd just learned. Bob came back, shaking his head ruefully.

"I thought I'd have to knock him out and toss his body onto the walk for pickup by his friends," he remarked. "In case you were wondering how effective that dress is, I'd say you now know."

"It better be effective," Laine said with a distracted smile. "After what I paid for it, it ought to cause explosions."

Bob was looking very handsome and formal in black tie, and to complement his simple elegance Laine had chosen the most spectacular gown she'd brought with her. It was a shade of green that enhanced the color of her eyes, the fabric a clinging chiffon modestly highlighted with matching sequins. The halter top left her shoulders and arms bare, the low-cut bodice exposed an impressive amount of cleavage, and the skirt didn't begin to flare almost until it had reached her ankles. Her necklace and long earrings were set with diamonds, as was the matching bracelet. Shoes and bag went with the gown, and wearing her hair long and loose completed the effect. The deputy had looked poleaxed when he'd first seen her, and it had taken him some effort to get down to business.

"Laine, don't let what you heard bother you," Bob said, that heavy control still obvious in his voice. "I said I'd be with you at all times from now on, and I wasn't joking."

"Don't you think you'll be the least bit conspicuous in public ladies' rooms?" Laine asked, turning to him with wide-eyed innocence. "Maybe you ought to carry a skirt and a wig for those occasions, just to keep riots from starting. Any man caught in a ladies' room is fair game, you know, so—"

"Will you please stop that," he interrupted with a sigh. "I know you're not thinking of this as a game, so save the lighthearted comedy routine for your series role. You have a right to be frightened, so stop trying to hide it."

"I think I'm more disturbed than frightened," Laine said, still trying to get her friend to lighten up. "Why did my attackers only want to rough me up? Doesn't that strike you as odd?"

"Not necessarily," Bob disagreed. "If you were hurt only a little, it would simply get you to *stop* what you were doing. Or maybe the guy who hired those two is a fan of yours."

"Some fan," she answered with a snort. "I prefer the ones who want autographs rather than blood. But why would anyone want me to stop what I'm doing? It isn't as if I'm picking up secrets and clues by the gross. So far I haven't learned anything."

"As far as *you* know," Bob pointed out. "And that doesn't count what you might learn in the future. Why don't we just have a pleasant night out tonight, and leave detective work for some other time?"

"And let them think they scared me off?" Laine demanded, then shook her head grimly. "No, I'm not that easy to scare off. And I *want* the one who killed Nissa to try to attack me. If and when that happens, I'll be ready."

"And I'll be a nervous wreck," he muttered, staring at her darkly. "Not to mention old and gray. I don't understand what you have against being scared off. Doesn't it beat being dead? What if I turn my head at the wrong minute, and somebody finishes the job that was started this afternoon? With all my black suits in the cleaner's, I won't have anything to wear to a funeral."

"Since the funeral won't be mine, we can both wear shocking pink," Laine told him, finding it impossible to smile. "I'm going to get him, her or it, Bob, not let them get me. If you never believe anything else in your life, I want you to believe *that*."

"I think I do believe it," he said slowly, then gave her a smile. "Okay, tiger, let's go get 'em. And I hope your boyfriend shows up to give me a hand. I have a feeling I'll need it."

"*I'll* be there to give you a hand, and he's not my boyfriend," Laine grumbled. "Besides, if he shows up he'll probably get in my way. He's involved in this mess somehow, but he doesn't want me to be."

"Well, then, that proves his guilt," Bob said, beginning to lead the way to the door. "It's the only reason *I* can think of for a man to want a woman to stay out of trouble. He can't possibly be worried about you."

Laine ignored Bob's sarcasm as she followed him, determined to close the subject of Greg Williams. She'd been fighting thoughts of him since that afternoon, but every time she blinked he was back again. The look of fury in his pale blue eyes as he hit the man who had attacked her, the gentle way he had held her to his big, powerful body—and the pain she had seen when she'd accused him of being responsible for the attack.

Someone who was involved in all that had no business looking hurt, Laine told herself firmly as she stepped outside. Some people could look hurt at the drop of a stage direction, but Laine had enough experience as an actress to know the real thing. Greg Williams had really been upset, and she was the one responsible.

"Which means I'll never be able to think of what to say to him," she muttered too low for Bob to hear. "If he shows up tonight I'll want to go into hiding."

"Did you say something?" Bob asked, coming up to walk beside her.

"Just praying a little," Laine answered with a sigh. "Let's not dawdle over dinner. The sooner we're through, the quicker we can get started."

"Oh, boy. I can hardly wait," he responded with no enthusiasm at all, but stayed right with her even as she laughed at him.

Dinner in the Silk Room wasn't as pleasant as eating in the Velvet Room had been. The service was slower, the waiters were graduate snobs, and the menu was in French. Laine was so annoyed she ordered a cheeseburger and fries, just to watch the expression on their waiter's face. Bob was so busy looking suspiciously around he didn't notice, not until the head waiter came over to beg Laine to change her order.

When they finally made their escape after dinner, Laine was more than ready to get on with the real reason she was there. The Show Room was already darkened for the performance that had started just a few minutes ago, the show girls strutting around in elaborate costumes while a handsome man with a microphone sang to the audience. After that the stand-up comics were on, which meant the people in the audience were effectively out of reach until the show was over.

"Looks like we'll have to start with the guests in the casino," Laine concluded to Bob as they walked away from the Show Room doors. "Not that I'm disappointed. Most of the people I could see watching the show looked familiar, which means I've probably already spoken to them."

"And what we're looking for is *new* blood," Bob said with a nod in a very sober tone. "Sounds delicious."

"We're after a werewolf, not a vampire, Bob," Laine corrected absently. "Let's try to keep the side comments appropriate, okay?"

"If I used the appropriate comments now, you'd never speak to me again," he muttered, looking all around rather than at her. "Are we starting with the anteroom, or going directly into the casino?"

"The anteroom," Laine answered. The anteroom to the casino sounded as if it would be small, but it wasn't.

"It looks like you have your work cut out for you," Bob murmured as they walked through the velvet-draped doors. "This is a larger crowd than I was expecting. Do you want a drink?"

"I think we'd both better get one," Laine returned, looking around at all the well-dressed people. A surprising number were dancing to the music, but the majority were engaged in easy conversation. "We've got the new blood you were interested in, so the show is about to start."

Bob's groan was low but sincere, and Laine smiled as she led the way to the bar. He'd been able to escape that afternoon, but right now he was stuck.

As soon as they had their drinks, they began circulating. Laine was recognized immediately by most of the people there, but happily they considered rushing at a star to be beneath them. That didn't mean they didn't greet her eagerly when she approached them, or that they weren't flattered when she asked for their help in her investigation. People enjoyed the thought of associating with a celebrity, no matter how unusual her interest.

The first group of people she spoke to were of no help at all, but Laine's step quickened as she approached the second group. One of the men was the guest who had, along with a woman, found the bodies, and Laine wanted to question him. The deputy who had taken his statement had asked almost nothing at all.

Laine introduced herself in the usual way, pretending no one there knew who she was. The ploy let her launch directly into *why* she was there, and was designed to catch people off guard. Up to that point it hadn't worked too well, but this time luck was with her.

"Say, if you're investigating this thing, you need to talk to Don here," one of the men offered, gesturing to the man he meant with his glass. "He and Sassy were the ones who found the bodies."

"No, really?" Laine said as if she hadn't known that, turning delighted eyes on the man called Don. "You *must* tell me all about it."

"Sassy just went back to our suite," Don said with the oddest expression. "She's been a nervous wreck ever since the murders. I'm Donald Meerson, by the way. We met briefly about a year ago. Ever since then I've been one of your biggest fans."

Don Meerson was showing an idolizing smile, and offering a handshake that was excitedly shy. Laine let him take her hand while she studied him, trying to remember his receding brown hairline, mild brown eyes and very slight paunch. He could have been anywhere in age from late forties to late fifties, and there was nothing at all distinctive about him.

"Oh, yes, now I remember," Laine lied, giving the man a smile of her own. "I don't recall where, but I do remember the face. And isn't it lucky that an old friend of mine was the one to be first on the crime scene? Tell me everything, Don, especially if it sounds strange. Did you and Sassy see something you couldn't quite bring yourselves to tell the police?"

"All we saw was those two poor people, lying dead on the ground near the call box we were going to use," the man answered with a sigh. "It didn't occur to me until later, but if we'd come by just a few minutes earlier, those bodies could have been *us*. If the police were letting people leave . . ."

"Hey, Don, tell her what Sassy's been saying," the first man directed with a grin. "The girl keeps saying it no matter how many times she's laughed at."

"Give me a break, Ralph," Don Meerson said with a grimace, now looking embarrassed and a bit upset. "All Sassy claims is that she saw a shadow, which probably came from her imagination."

"What kind of shadow did she see?" Laine asked, pretending she wasn't aware of Don's discomfort. "Come on, Ralph, *you* tell me."

"The girl is ready to swear she saw a really grotesque shadow on the ground just before she and Don ran for help," Ralph answered without hesitation. "She won't describe the shadow, but she says she saw it. The police asked if it was man-shaped, and when she said no they didn't ask anything else."

"She told that to the police?" Laine said with surprise she wasn't feeling. "Then why didn't they tell *me*? Don, do you think I could talk to Sassy myself? Even for just a minute or two?"

"Well, maybe tomorrow," the man grudged after a brief hesitation, looking really unhappy. "She gets so wild and nervous when anyone tries to question her. As though she were afraid to go into real detail. I'll ask her, and if she's willing I'll call your suite."

"Oh, thank you, Don," Laine gushed, putting a hand to his arm. "If you can arrange it, I'll be grateful forever. Are you sure *you* didn't see anything?"

"Only those bodies," he replied shaking his head, but he was smiling again. "Now I wish I had. Would you have dinner with me tomorrow night? I'm having a small party at my suite, and we could talk about your career and what you plan to do next."

"I'll check my schedule and let you know tomorrow," she answered with smiling warmth, then excused herself to go on to the next group. She hadn't wanted to discourage the man by turning him down completely, since she needed to talk to Sassy. Having dinner at a party with him would be a small price if his lady friend had anything really worthwhile to say.

Three more groups were visited with nothing to show for the effort, but Laine didn't get to continue on to the next. Bob stopped her once they were beyond the closest ears, and he looked annoyed with himself.

"I really hate saying this, but I've got to make a quick trip to the men's room," he told her, explaining the annoyance. "I want you to give me your word that you'll wait right here even if there's an Indian attack complete with fire arrows. Not an inch from here. I swear I'll get back as fast as I can."

"That seems to mean you don't want me to go with you," Laine said in a faintly disappointed way. "Why don't you get us fresh drinks on the way back."

He glared at her as he took the glass she held out, then left without commenting. Laine didn't particularly mind the break. The air-conditioning was doing a reasonable job of keeping the richly decorated room cool, but—

"See? You missed it," a voice said from behind her left shoulder, causing her to turn. It was the heckler from the pool area that afternoon, now wearing black tie rather than brief swim trunks. Laine remembered his name was Jeremy Roberts.

"If you expect me to ask what I missed, you're wasting your time," she said, turning away from him again. That was all she intended to say, but apparently the man was still into not giving up.

"What you missed was having dinner with a man who would have paid attention to *you* rather than everyone else," he told her anyway, moving around to face her again. "Now that he's gone, I'm here to show you the difference. I'll walk around *with* you rather than behind you, and you can talk to *me* instead of to other people. Let's go."

"I'm a lot stronger than you seem to think," Laine told him, ignoring the arm he held out to her. "Threatening a fate that horrible might intimidate other women, but I tend to laugh in the face of threats. Now go away."

"I love how witty you are," he said with a grin, his hand on her arm keeping her from turning away again. "I think I'll show you the terrace first, and then we can go on from there. Breakfast's an even better meal to share than dinner."

"Stop being an idiot and let go of my arm," Laine snapped, finding that a simple pull hadn't been able to free her. "I'm not even enjoying sharing this planet with you. If this dress wasn't so tight—"

"I noticed how tight it was myself," he interrupted, the grin still going strong. "Now don't make a scene, or I'll have to tell everyone how you encouraged me. The scandal sheets will love the story, but your producers won't. The terrace is right out there."

And with that he began forcing her toward the closed and curtained doors at the rear of the room.

Chapter Twelve

Greg Williams had dinner supplied by room service, but it was a solitary meal. Anita was on her way to do a chore for him. He glanced again at some of the background files as he ate, but he and Anita had pretty much stripped them dry. There wasn't yet a file for everyone at the hotel, but his people had made a good beginning.

And now he knew why the sheriff had listened to Laine Randall. The fact that she'd helped Hollywood PD solve three major crimes hadn't been publicized, but it was certainly a matter of record. She seemed to be good at picking up subtle clues and interpreting them correctly, at picking out the false note in a symphony of excuses.

Which explained why she'd noticed *him* so quickly. Of all the people he could have jostled at the train station, he'd had to pick the one who would notice he wasn't what he claimed to be. Professionally speaking it had been a bad mistake, but considering it on a more personal level . . .

It might still turn out to be a mistake. He'd learned something else about Laine Randall that had to be discussed with her, and the exchange wasn't going to

be a pleasant one. It was just possible she wasn't seeing the forest for the trees, and Greg didn't expect her
to thank him for pointing out branches and leaves.
She'd be much more likely to—

"I'm back," Anita announced, having let herself in
with her passkey card. "The light of your life and her
secretary had a reservation for dinner in the Silk
Room. Was there something wrong with the food?"

"If I wait too long to eat, I lose my appetite," Greg
said, pushing away the plate he'd been mostly staring
at. "I'll make up for it at breakfast. Right now I'd
better get dressed."

"Isn't it lucky you just *happen* to travel with the
appropriate wardrobe," Anita observed as he left the
table. "Or is black tie part of standard issue for men
at your level?"

"Standard issue," he answered over his shoulder
with a laugh. "You'd be surprised how often we're
required to go formal. But next level it gets even better. You qualify for a bullet-proof cummerbund."

"Just when you don't need it any more," Anita said
with a laugh of her own. "Typical. Do you want me
to get those reports together and put them anywhere
in particular?"

"In my luggage," Greg instructed with a nod.
"That won't keep them from the sheriff and a search
warrant, but any casual callers I might get won't find
them as easily. And I just *might* have company. I'm
going to start being very conspicuous."

"You're going to use yourself as bait?" Anita
asked, immediately disturbed. "Greg, is that wise?
They already have two dead bodies to their credit.
Three won't make any difference at all."

"Turning me into a dead body isn't all that easy," he told her with a smile. "I'm sure you know it's been tried before. And besides, I'll have you backing me up, won't I? Did you find out which rooms in this immediate area are empty?"

"The one across the hall on the right is available," she answered with a nod. "The one on the left is occupied so I'll have to be very quiet, but—"

"But you can be, so there won't be a problem," he concluded for her. "And now I really do have to get dressed. Just remember there won't be anyone backing *you* up, so don't take any chances at all. If you see someone come in here, don't try coming in after them alone. If I'm not back in time, just remember their face and let them go."

"Yes, sir," she muttered, turning away from him in annoyance. "Whatever you say, sir."

Greg grinned as he carried his clothes into the bathroom. Anita was very unhappy with him, but she would still obey his orders. It helped having a woman like her in a position where she had to obey. All he had to do now was figure out a way to put Laine Randall in a similarly safe position.

By the time he was dressed, Anita had taken care of the reports and had left the room. He checked the clip on his 9MM automatic, holstered the weapon in his pants at the small of his back under his jacket, then left the room himself. He was tempted to wave at Anita where she undoubtedly watched him through the peephole across the way, but that wouldn't have been smart. If no one had seen her go in there, only an amateur would have pointed her out.

It wasn't very long before Greg was downstairs and in the midst of a large number of expensively dressed people. Most of them were heading for the casino, and Greg strolled along with them, camouflaging his presence with theirs. He would look for Laine in the casino first, and if she wasn't there he would try the Show Room. Eventually he would find her, and then they would have their talk.

Greg was almost surprised to find that his luck seemed to have returned. Laine Randall was in the casino anteroom, talking to a bunch of people while her friend stood silently behind her. He moved to the opposite side of the room where he could see without being seen, needing to stand there for a while and simply stare.

She had to be the most incredible woman he'd ever come across, and not only because of the way she looked. She was breathtaking in a gown of green that glimmered when she moved, the material of it hugging her marvelous curves all the way down. She wore her midnight hair loose as usual, and it flowed down her back and around her shoulders in a way that turned his mouth dry.

But she was also talking to the people she stood with, reaching out to them with the strength of her personality. The words she used didn't matter; it was *her* they were responding to, *her* they were being drawn to. Whatever she was asking, they would give it to her without the least hesitation.

And the thought of what she could be asking for turned his mouth even drier. Greg knew without any doubt that she was there investigating. She was asking for information in a way even the police couldn't do, and most likely everyone would talk to her. But the danger that put her in was enough to turn his hair gray.

Damn it, had she already forgotten about that afternoon? Greg could feel the burning fury rise up in him again when he remembered the attacker who had tried to hurt her, but the significance of the episode had apparently escaped *her*. Someone besides himself wanted her to stop snooping, but apparently she didn't believe in cooperating with anyone.

Through smouldering anger Greg watched as she left the group she was with. She had a brief conversation with Robert Samson, then he carried their glasses away. The big, dark-haired man put both down on an empty table he passed, then left the room. He was going somewhere, and it might be helpful to know just where.

But that would leave Laine without anyone to keep an eye on her. Granted she was in a room full of people who couldn't all be guilty of murder, and if she needed help all she would have to do was shout. She ought to be safe enough, and although Greg had begun moving after her big friend, he was already out of sight. Greg would have to hurry if he was going to catch up, but one last glance at Laine...

Which was all it took. Laine Randall's arm was being held in a way she would normally never stand for, and the man doing it was using that hold to force her to walk with him. Greg didn't know what was going on, but all thoughts of following Robert Samson disappeared. There was something more important that needed doing.

He made his way quickly through the milling crowd, only just avoiding knocking people down. He came up behind Laine and the man without either of them seeing him, and at that point Laine was speaking.

"...care *what* the scandal sheets want to print," she growled, using her body weight to resist being forced ahead. "You have five seconds to let go of me, and if you don't I'll knock those perfect teeth right out of your face."

"Why do you have to be so unfriendly?" the man complained, sounding really put-upon. "Everyone knows actresses do it with anybody who's important enough. I have a lot of money to invest, and I'm thinking about putting it into a movie..."

"Then you'll need a lot of popcorn," Greg said, reaching over to take the man's arm by the pressure point just above the elbow. "You know, to go with the movie. Why don't you leave right now to order it?"

"Ow, you're hurting my arm!" the man complained, having let go of Laine as soon as his own arm was taken. "And who the hell are you to barge into a private conversation? We were just—"

"You were just leaving," Greg interrupted again, his voice very soft. "Say good night to the lady."

The smaller man looked into Greg's eyes, swallowed hard, then nodded with a jerk of his head. His tan seemed to have paled just a little, but Greg felt no pity for him. He was garbage, and deserved whatever he got.

"I'll—I'll come back some other time, Laine," he managed in a croak, then stepped back before walking away. He was obviously trying to maintain his supposed dignity, but that was hard to do while rubbing at a bruised arm.

Greg watched to make sure the glamour boy didn't change his mind about coming back, but while he watched he became aware of the heavy silence behind him to his left. He turned to find Laine Randall staring at him, her unbelievable green eyes filled with a very odd expression.

"Are you all right?" Greg asked her, and then a disturbing thought came to him. "I didn't storm in where I wasn't wanted, did I? I mean, he *was* giving you a hard time . . . ?"

"He *thought* he was giving me a hard time," she corrected, but something of a smile accompanied the words. "I have a lot of experience with creeps like that, and he wouldn't have gotten what he expected to." Then her smile disappeared entirely. "But you did save me from having to do it myself, and that makes twice. Are you going to keep it up until I learn how to thank you properly?"

"If necessary," he agreed with a judicious nod. "I happen to believe everybody should know how to say a proper thank-you, so my duty is clear. You wouldn't want me to shirk my duty, would you?"

"Heaven forbid," she answered, with a firm shake of her head. "If it ever got out that I made a man shirk his duty—at the very least, my career would be in tatters."

"Then I have to keep it up for both our sakes," Greg said. He hesitated briefly, wondering if the time was right, then took the coward's way. "Would you dance with me? Just for this one song? It happens to be a favorite of mine."

"All right," she agreed after a short hesitation of her own, then led the way to the polished wood dance floor. He followed right behind, and when she turned to face him he immediately took her in his arms. "By the way, what song *is* this?" she added.

"I have no idea," he answered with a grin, delighting in the softness of the hand he held in his own.

"Whatever it is, though, from now on it will be a favorite of mine."

"You're impossible," she pronounced, then grinned. "But the least I owe you is a dance. While we're at it, I'll be trying to think of a graceful way to apologize."

"For what?" Greg asked, his hand on her back slowly bringing her closer to him. Her perfume was very subtle, but now that he was aware of it he felt his body beginning to stir. The least he wanted to do was close his eyes and breathe deeply, but if he ever did...

"For accusing you of having staged the attack this afternoon," she answered with a sigh. "Saying it straight out like that isn't very graceful, but it *is* sincere. Even if the thugs don't know who *did* hire them, it isn't logical for the unknown boss to be you."

"Ah, then it's logic I have to thank for being declared innocent," he said, wishing she would look up at him. "The sheriff told you what he got out of questioning that pair?"

"One of his deputies came by with the meager results." When she nodded her affirmation her hair slid over her shoulders, making Greg wonder what it would be like to touch that bare skin with his lips. "If you were the guilty one, you wouldn't have interfered until they'd done their job. They were supposed to hurt me a little."

"Hurt you," Greg echoed, suddenly working very hard to control his rage. "But just a little. Was that your qualification, or theirs?"

"Theirs," she answered, and now she *did* look up at him. "What's wrong?"

"I don't like the implications of those orders," he said, most of his pleasure from moving to the romantic music gone. "Does the sheriff know there's a man here with a record of violent crime? An ex-con, in fact?"

"Who told you that?" she demanded immediately, stiffening in his arms. "If that's the trail you're on, you'd better recheck your map. The only place it leads is to a dead end."

"What good do you think it will do to shield him?" Greg quietly asked the blaze coming at him from furious green eyes. "Robert Amberon—not Robert Samson—spent time behind bars for aggravated assault. At his size, he's lucky it didn't turn out to be manslaughter. There are two people dead, Laine, so stop to think about it. Don't tell me you can't see how easily the attack on you fits the facts."

"How did you find out about Bob?" she demanded again, no longer moving to the music. "I *have* thought about the facts, and I know him well enough to know he isn't involved in this. Who are you to suggest that he is? *Who* are you?"

Greg loved her fierce loyalty to a friend, but this simply wasn't the time for it. She was starting to hate him again because he'd mentioned Robert Samson, and he didn't want that to happen. He parted his lips, prepared to divert her from who and what he was, when it came to him that everyone had stopped dancing.

"What's going on?" Laine asked with a frown, noticing the same thing he had. "Why is everyone so excited?"

"I don't know," Greg answered, seeing that the source of the agitation was closer to the anteroom entrance. "Let's go find out."

They left the dance floor and made their way toward the milling, chattering crowd, and then they heard the news.

The werewolf had killed two more people.

Chapter Thirteen

"This time, at least, they were both members of the staff," Laine mimicked. "The management of this place must be delighted with that. Paying guests should be off limits."

"Yes, I got that from the scattered comments myself," Greg acknowledged with a sigh. "None of them seem to have noticed that two more human beings are dead. As long as guests are being left alone, they're enjoying standing back and watching the entertainment."

"Well, I don't consider it entertainment," Laine snarled, pushing into her suite as soon as the lock turned green. "There has to be something wrong with those people."

She and Greg had spent too much time standing with the group staring at the latest victims, and the comments she'd heard had been more sickening than the sight of shredded, lifeless bodies.

"Did you notice how close to the first murder scene that second one was?" Greg asked as he followed her into the living room. "It had to have been done in between the rounds of the discreet patrol the sheriff set up. Once again it was a man and a woman. I wonder if that's nothing but a coincidence.''

Laine stopped in the middle of the room to hug herself against an inner chill. Once again she was seeing Nissa lying there, lifeless eyes staring, poor little body savaged and tossed away. The pouring rain should have made the staring eyes blink but it hadn't, and Laine would remember noticing that to her dying day.

''It's so much harder when you're personally involved,'' Greg said in a murmur. And then his arms were wrapped around her, drawing her close to his warmth and steadiness. ''You become determined to find out who did it, but you can't stop the pain while you're looking.''

''You sound like you're speaking from personal experience,'' Laine said with her cheek to his dress shirt, needing the contact very badly.

''I am,'' he admitted, the hand on her bare back unmoving. ''A very close friend of mine was killed, and I went looking for his murderer. When I finally caught up to the one who had done it, I found it was another very close friend of ours. And I would have found him sooner if I'd been willing to admit that such a thing was possible.''

''You still think Bob is involved,'' Laine said with a weary sigh, too depressed to pull away from his hold. ''Can't you accept my word that you're wrong?''

''Your word is too emotionally involved,'' he returned in a very gentle way. ''Are you in love with him? Is that why you're so sure he's innocent?''

Laine leaned back to look up at Greg, and unless she was completely mistaken the man was just about holding his breath. He'd asked a question he didn't want to hear the answer to, not if that answer had the chance of being yes.

"All right, I've had enough of this," she stated, more for her own benefit than his. "I want to know who you are, which will hopefully tell me why any of this is your business. Start talking, buster, or else."

"Or else what?" he asked, blinking as he looked down at her. "I hope you'll excuse my confusion. I'm not used to being threatened by junior G-men."

"Then it's about time you had the experience," she returned with a laugh, stepping back from his loosened hold. "The sheriff picked you up for questioning on my say so, but he let you go again. It's come to me that if he found nothing suspicious about you, he would have made sure to tell me. Since he *didn't* but still let you go, it's fairly safe to assume he found something he was discouraged from discussing."

"Logic as shaky as that shouldn't be relied on," he answered, no expression at all on his face. "Don't you know what can happen if you assume things?"

"And then, completely out of the blue, you come up with not only Bob's record, but his real name," Laine went on as though Greg hadn't said a word. "All that put together tells me certain things, but I want details. If I don't get them, I guarantee everyone at this resort will have heard about my guesswork by lunchtime tomorrow."

"That's blackmail," he growled, a hard look now in his eyes. "And if I *am* who you think I am, trying to blackmail me could get you locked up somewhere until this is all over."

"But that's just the point," she countered, still amused. "I don't *know* who you are, so all I can do is guess. And if I should happen to be locked up for no reason, *you'll* end up being very sorry. Once free, I'd hold a press conference, the sort that would have *you* on the carpet with your head on a platter. Wouldn't it be much easier just telling me what I want to know?''

"It would be easiest committing a murder of my own," he answered darkly as he folded his arms. "I could simply walk out of here and let you tell people anything you like. How many of them will believe a woman who's investigating werewolves?''

"Probably not many," Laine granted with a grin. "Maybe just the ones you came here after. And you *were* following someone when you got here, I'm certain of that now.''

He stood staring down at her, heavy annoyance in those very light eyes, but he'd stopped arguing. Or, he'd stopped arguing with *her*. He was clearly in the middle of a debate with himself, but Laine wasn't worried. There was only one intelligent decision he could come to, which he did after another moment.

"If any of this gets out, I won't have to worry about committing murder," he warned. "I'll be investigating oddities in foreign salt mines, and you'll be too busy defending yourself in court to have any career left. If, that is, the terrorists don't get to us first. Do you understand me?''

"Terrorists?" Laine echoed, all amusement suddenly gone. "You don't mean you came here chasing terrorists?''

"Not exactly," he answered with a sigh. "Let's sit down and I'll start from the beginning.''

He gestured to the nearest couch, then followed Laine over to it. He also seemed to be thinking about how it would be best to start, so Laine didn't complain about the delay. As soon as they were settled, he made up his mind.

"About a month ago, one of our operatives started picking up odd bits and pieces in connection with a terrorist group called the Morescu," he began. "They're one of the most dangerous organizations around because they aren't politically or religiously motivated. They're in it for money and power, and therefore can pick and choose what they become involved in. They don't get caught in awkward situations while leaving messages for the world to take note of; they work quietly and efficiently, and collect their payoffs without a fuss."

"Just a minute," Laine interrupted. "You said one of your operatives. You still haven't told me who you are."

"Interpol," he replied, then smiled at her expression. "Or were you expecting me to be part of Dr. No's organization?"

"I was thinking more along domestic lines," Laine admitted, still feeling the flush in her cheeks from the surprise she'd shown. "Go on with your story."

"What we learned was that the Morescu was involved with some American group, and had a high cash deal going with them. It would have been nice having a few details on the deal, but the Morescu could teach the CIA and KGB lessons in security silence. We were able to identify one of their couriers, so we followed him hoping he would lead us to a meet. I picked him up at Kennedy Airport in New York, and followed him here." At that point, Greg shrugged. "He was the man who was murdered last night with your friend."

"But that doesn't make any sense," Laine objected, feeling the mind picture she'd been building suddenly fall apart. "The man comes here for dark business reasons, and just *happens* to become one of the victims of a werewolf? Most things are possible I suppose, but it isn't very likely."

"And yet it is still possible," Greg pointed out. "I can't imagine where this werewolf business fits in, but if the courier was trying to make contact with someone here, he could very well have been in the wrong place at the wrong time."

"So that's why you suspect Bob," Laine said, seeing in his eyes what he *hadn't* said. "You think the courier was here to meet Nissa, and she and Bob were both involved with him. I'm sorry, but that simply won't work."

"Why not?" Greg asked gently, putting out one big hand to smooth her hair. "I know how you felt about your friend, but no one can know everything about another person. It's possible only Robert Amberon is a major player, and he forced your friend to go along with him."

"That's even more unlikely," Laine answered with a sigh. "How can I explain to you—look, I'm an actress. At various times I've had to portray every emotion and feeling there is, but it's never been a case of choosing-what-you-like-best. The emotions and reactions of my role character have to fit the situation, otherwise they stand out like fluorescent colors. You always have to use what fits—which means you have to *know* what fits and what doesn't."

"And being involved with terrorists doesn't fit your friends?" Greg asked kindly. "Don't you realize it never fits anyone until the minute it can no longer be denied?"

"Stop being so damned understanding and listen," Laine growled, beginning to be very annoyed with his noble patience. "If you told me your major evidence of something was carefully hidden in a very small crawl space somewhere, would you also be able to tell me that your major suspect was a violent claustrophobic? Would it be possible for someone who was violently afraid of being closed in, to hide something carefully in a small, crowded space?"

"Not if you stress the word *carefully*," he conceded with a frown. "Thrown in, yes; carefully hidden, no. A claustrophobic would never choose a hiding place like that."

"And someone who was violently afraid of real life would never get involved with secret plots," Laine stated. "You don't get involved in things like that to do absolutely nothing, and that's all Nissa would have been able to do. She could handle things if they were *my* things, but never her own. And if anyone had tried forcing her into anything, her behavior would have been so erratic even strangers would have noticed. *I* would have seen it immediately."

"What if she was being used without her knowledge?" Greg came back, conceding the point by coming up with another. "Robert Amberon could have asked her to do him a favor, and doing it got her accidently killed. Or incidently killed. Maybe Amberon knew that whoever met Lundgren would end up dead."

"But that would mean Bob was actively involved, and I still don't believe that," Laine said with a violent shake of her head. "And more than that, it would mean he *used* Nissa, something he could never do. We're wasting time on a dead end—"

"Why?" Greg demanded, those light eyes hard again as he moved closer. "You still haven't answered my question. Are you that sure of his innocence because you're in love with him? Just what is he to you?"

"I'm...not...in love with him," Laine stumbled, suddenly very uncomfortable under that hard-eyed stare. "And it isn't a matter of what he is to me. It's what I am to him."

"Which is?" Greg prompted, his expression unchanging.

"Damn it, stop looking at me like that!" Laine protested, one step short of squirming. "I'm his Chinese Obligation."

The stare coming down at her wavered, and then blond brows rose over confused blue eyes.

"Would you repeat that?" he asked. "Preferably in this language?"

"I'm his Chinese Obligation," Laine repeated with a sigh. "I first met Bob under unusual circumstances. We were supposed to do some street shooting for the series, but I couldn't leave for the location with the rest of the crew. I was scheduled to tape a talk show, then would meet everyone afterward. My then secretary had taken down the address of where I was supposed to go."

"And it turned out to be the wrong address," Greg guessed, not precisely a blind intuitive leap.

"What else?" Laine confirmed with a shrug. "After watching my taxi drive away as fast as it could go, I looked around and understood why. There was no sign of the crew, something I should have noticed before getting out of the cab. I also hadn't noticed that *I'd* been noticed.''

Laine paused briefly, once more feeling the fear from that time grip her, but less sharply than it once had. She would never forget it, but she'd managed to conquer a good part of the terror.

"Three men tried to show their admiration by dragging me into a nearby building,'' she told Greg with a faint smile. "Back then I knew nothing about unarmed combat. All fighting in the series was done by my stunt double. I wouldn't have had a chance if Bob hadn't interfered, taking on all three of them and starting a riot. When the police got there they tried to arrest Bob along with the three attackers. He was out on parole, you see, and shouldn't have gotten involved in a street fight. I was so mad I almost did some attacking of my own, with the police as my victims.''

"But instead you got him cleared of any charges and gave him a job,'' Greg said, this time not guessing. "I can understand you being grateful to him, but—''

"No, you *don't* understand,'' Laine interrupted in exasperation. "The only reason he took the job I offered was because he felt responsible for me. His pride tried to make him refuse a 'gratitude' job, but saving me meant he was responsible for me from then on. That's called a Chinese Obligation, and I want you to stop and think about it. What sort of man *accepts* a thing like that? The same sort of man who could deal with terrorists and send a helpless girl to her death? Or a man who has a very strict code of honor, and in any event isn't stupid. Bob has a normal, successful life right in his reach. Why would he jeopardize that?''

"Blackmail?'' Greg suggested at once, unimpressed with her explanation. "If that normal, successful life was threatened, or if instead someone close to him was threatened . . . You did say he considered himself responsible for you. What if they threatened to kill *you* if he didn't cooperate?"

"Now you're reaching," Laine said with a derisive snort. "If he was being blackmailed, I would have noticed something in his attitude. All we're doing is going round and round in circles that lead nowhere."

"It doesn't seem possible to do anything else on this case," Greg muttered, then looked straight at her again. "You still don't have me convinced, but there are other things to talk about. You forced information out of me, and for that you owe me something. Am I wrong in believing you have copies of the sheriff's file of the investigation?"

"No, you're not," Laine agreed, happy to get his mind off Bob. "I have the complete file in my bedroom. Why don't you have your own copy of it?"

"Because the sheriff doesn't know exactly who I'm working for," he answered promptly. "I showed him enough to give him a reason to release me, but not enough to share his investigation results. I wasn't kidding about what could happen if the wrong people find out about my background. Will you show me the file?"

"I don't know," Laine temporized, tapping her lips with one finger. "That file is supposed to be confidential. I'd have to have an awfully good reason for sharing it with you... Oh, say, like your promise to let *me* see the information your people have gathered. If you have a file on Bob, it stands to reason there are others . . ."

"Damn it, woman, how many times do you think you can blackmail me?" he demanded, and abruptly he was even closer than he had been. "If you need a reason for cooperating, how about this?"

His arms were around her even before he finished speaking, and then their lips were together the way they'd been once before. This time, though, he wasn't holding back, and Laine felt herself responding instantly. There was something about this man that had attracted her from the first, and the angry passion of his kiss was like something she'd been waiting for for a very long time.

But the angry part didn't last long. When her arms slipped around to his back and she parted her lips for him, he murmured a sound that was deep pleasure and caressed her tongue with his. His hands were also moving slowly on her back and bottom, the beginnings of a different sort of investigation that he'd been waiting to start.

Laine loved the taste and touch of his mouth, but she had to pull back before it got beyond her control. "That's a very compelling reason to cooperate," she gasped, finding it hard to avoid the feather-light kisses he followed her with. "The only problem is—Greg, will you please stop that?—the problem is I'm in the middle of an investigation. I can't just give up my assets, I have to trade them where they'll do the most good."

"Mmm, yes, an investigation," he murmured, leaning over her while his hand stroked down her thigh. "And you do have assets, the most wonderful ones I've ever seen. Trading them is a marvelous idea, I'm all for it. My own assets aren't anywhere near as good, but they're all yours. Let's trade right now."

"Greg, I'm talking about the information I have," Laine said desperately, her eyes fluttering closed when his hand reached under her gown and began to rise slowly up her leg. "We—we have to trade *that,* not—"

Her disjointed words were cut off when his lips took hers again, and Laine was very much afraid she was lost. The biggest problem was that she *wanted* to be lost, whether or not now was the time for it, whether or not there were still things to be done. She wanted Greg Williams with an intensity that was almost frightening; that he obviously wanted her as badly simply reinforced her feelings.

And then, with the abruptness of a rude awakening, the suite door was opened and closed with a slam.

Chapter Fourteen

Laine jumped like a teenager caught by the unexpected return of her parents, and Greg released her so fast he must have been thinking the same thing. She saw his hand begin to move under his jacket toward his back, and then she saw a completely furious Bob.

"So there you are!" he stormed, glaring down at her with his fists to his hips. "Have you any idea what you just put me through? I was picturing you lying dead somewhere, and instead I find you necking in a corner!"

"Bob, please," Laine tried, blushing like that teenager she'd been thinking about. "It's not—"

"First someone locks me in the men's room, and after pounding on the door for what feels like hours, I finally attract someone's attention. As soon as the door is opened I go flying back to the woman I'm supposed to be protecting, only to find her and almost everyone else gone! Two more people are dead, I'm told, and the general opinion is that the werewolf has struck again. Do you know how many years I aged until I saw that neither of the bodies was yours?"

"Bob, Greg came by just the way you were hoping he would," Laine interrupted hastily as she stood, putting one hand to his arm. "When we heard about the new murders we went to check the scene, and I was so upset Greg brought me back here. I'm sorry if you were worried, but I really didn't do it on purpose."

"You never do it on purpose," Bob returned darkly, refusing to be soothed. "But you still do it. And I had been thinking better of you, Williams."

With that observation he turned away from them and strode toward his bedroom. Laine flinched as the door slammed shut, then looked around to find Greg shaking his head wryly.

"Well, that puts me in *my* place," he muttered, one broad hand rubbing the back of his neck. "I don't think a suspect of mine has ever before told me I'm a disappointment to him. Do you think he'll ever let me date you again?"

"I'm still wondering if he'll send me to my room after grounding me," Laine answered with a grin. "You might have to find someone else to take to the prom."

"Since our kind of prom will have werewolves and murderers, that isn't the disappointment it could be," Greg countered. "I wonder why anyone would lock him in the men's room. If he *was* locked in. It gives him an odd sort of alibi for the time of the murder."

"And strangely enough, you were with *me* again," Laine immediately pointed out. "If you don't happen to be who you claim you are, that could be rather significant. Are we going to start suspecting each other again, or try to find out what's really going on?"

"Now you're threatening to suspect me again if I don't go along with you?" he asked with one brow raised. "Is blackmail a way of life with you, or are you doing this just for my benefit?"

"Well, I *have* been trying to make you feel more at home," Laine answered innocently. "You know, surrounded and outnumbered and under terrible pressure to come up with the right answer. Isn't that the way it usually goes for someone like you?"

"Happily, only in the movies," he returned with a snort. "And now that you mention it, I think I understand what I'm beginning to feel when I'm with you—surrounded and outnumbered."

"You forgot the part about being under terrible pressure, but maybe I can remind you." Laine's grin had a bit too much glee in it, but she did need to press the point. "If I show you mine, will you show me yours?"

"Isn't it lucky for you I know you mean the investigation files," Greg said with a laugh. "If Amberon had heard you, though, I'd probably be out on my ear and you'd be in big trouble. If that outrage he showed us is real, he's more than had it with you."

"I have nothing to worry about," Laine assured him. "If he tries to spank me, I get to dock his salary. Do we have a deal?"

"Do I have any other choice?" Greg countered. "There is one thing you'd better remember, though. Since I don't work for you, you can't dock *my* salary."

Despite the look in his very light eyes, Laine was certain he was joking. She cleared her throat, gave Greg something of a smile, then led the way to her bedroom.

The police file sent to her by the sheriff wasn't very thick, so it didn't take long for Greg to read through it. Laine sat in a chair while he sat in another with the paperwork, and it took some effort not to think about what had almost happened between them.

Now that they were no longer alone in the suite, Greg had joked about their closeness but hadn't tried to touch her again. No other man she'd ever met would have been that considerate of her, and the way it made her feel worried her. Could she really be getting serious about a man she still knew nothing about?

Not to mention the mess they were both neck deep in. There was a lot to consider in the little information Greg had given her, and those thoughts were even more disturbing. Terrorists were involved, and what were *they* up to . . . ?

"There's only one autopsy report here," Greg said, drawing her attention. "What about the one on your friend?"

"Apparently the coroner hadn't gotten to hers yet," Laine told him with a grimace. "They think she was killed only because she happened to be there."

"I know how you feel, but unfortunately that's more than possible," he said with a commiserating glance. "The male victim was 52 years of age, five feet, eight and one half inches tall, one hundred thirty-nine pounds. Hair brown, eyes brown, so on, so on…here it is. Death caused by a severed jugular vein, major point of attack lacerated rather than cut. There's no mention at all of what might have done the lacerating."

"You expected them to say, 'Victim apparently attacked by a werewolf'?" Laine asked. "The rest of the report doesn't even mention the paw print they found. If terrorists are a part of this, *why* are they involved? You said it was supposed to be a high cash deal. Which side is supplying the cash?"

"Well, it certainly isn't the Morescu," Greg answered with a snort. "If a terrorist group wants something, they steal it. Getting a bill of sale isn't of major concern to—ah, I see your point. If they're the ones with something to sell, they have to arrange to bring it into the country. Since we weren't able to find anything on their courier, he could have been bringing shipping arrangement information in his head. I wonder if he was killed before or after he passed on the details."

"If that's what he was here to do," Laine muttered, thinking about it. "I still don't understand why anyone would be dealing with terrorists. What could they possibly provide that couldn't be gotten more easily from others? Or am I wrong to believe the Morescu would take the money *without* delivering, and laugh as they did it? Do they have that high an international reputation to protect?"

"No, they have the usual terrorist reputation," Greg replied, frowning. "And while we're listing unanswered questions, how about this—why would they be bringing anything *into* this country? Their usual standard operating procedure is to *take* from a high-tech country, and sell to a backward one. And in any event, I withdraw the suggestion that their courier was bringing in information."

"Because it could have gotten here a lot more easily in other ways," Laine agreed with a nod. "I've already thought of that. On my series we once had a letter that was a major clue, but it meant nothing until it was decoded. The date on the letter provided the key to the reference volume used for the code, but each part by itself was useless to anyone who didn't know it all. The terrorists could have used the same trick more easily than sending a man.''

''Great,'' Greg said, tossing aside the file. ''We've just eliminated the only reasonable explanation for the man's being here. It's a good thing you weren't around in Sherlock Holmes's time. He probably would have ended up as a snack for the hounds of Baskerville.''

''Did that case come before or after the one with the Musgrave Ritual?'' Laine asked, looking at Greg with her head tilted to one side. ''I always loved the 'Musgrave Ritual,' and the way Basil Rathbone never let a little thing like a blank wall keep him from charging on.''

Light eyes met her gaze and stared back at her, and then he smiled at her.

''You're right, and I apologize,'' Greg murmured, leaving his chair to come over and crouch beside hers. ''It's not your fault we both eliminated my pet theory, and having nothing to go on doesn't mean we should give up. If you were there with Sherlock Holmes, the hounds of Baskerville wouldn't have *dared* to come near him.''

He took her hand and began kissing her fingers then, his eyes still looking up at her. Laine realized he was ready to apologize a lot more thoroughly than he already had, but with someone else in the suite *she* would have to be the one to lock the bedroom door. He had to know he could have influenced her decision by taking her in his arms again, but he had chosen not to.

He doesn't want me any way but completely willing, Laine thought to herself with surprise. *Until right now, I believed men like that were pure myth. Laine*

Randall, you have the world's worst luck when it comes to timing!

And she did. She still had something fairly important to do that night, but if she accepted Greg's invitation she wasn't likely to get to anything else. It almost killed her to do it, but she gently withdrew her tingling hand from his warm and tender grip.

"Maybe we'd better call it a night," she said, more grateful to her ability as an actress than he could possibly know. "Tomorrow we should have the file on tonight's murders, and while you go through that, I can look through your information. If none of it gives us any ideas, we'll just have to find one of these Morescu people and feed him some truth serum. What suite are you in?"

"Room," Greg corrected with a sigh, straightening as she stood. "It's room 322, and I guarantee if I get you in there, I'll have plenty of ideas. But don't let me discourage you from coming over anyway."

"Don't worry, you haven't," she told him, grinning at the innocent look he was giving her. "I can always bring a couple of deputies along to protect me."

"As long as it isn't your friend Bob," he said as he turned toward the door. "Deputies I can always bribe, or outrank . . . or overpower . . ."

"Good night!" Laine said with a laugh, shaking her head at the happy daydream expression he wore. "I'll see you tomorrow."

"You'd better believe it," he said, glancing at her one more time before leaving. Laine followed to make sure he was gone, then went back to her bedroom to sit down for a minute. She still had to change her clothes and finalize her plans, but first she wanted to enjoy the memory of that last look Greg had given her.

It had had so much promise in it, so very much promise.

WHEN GREG GOT BACK to his room he found Anita waiting there, and as soon as she looked at him her dark brows rose high.

"Let me guess," she said as he closed the door. "This time the rescuing hero didn't strike out. Am I right?"

"Close enough," he allowed with a grin. "The scenery is much nicer on second base. Why are you here instead of across the hall?"

"The police are all over the place," she answered with a shake of her head. "When I saw a bunch of them heading inside, I thought they might have decided to check empty rooms. It would be a good way to find out about intruders, so I got out of there. It's lucky I was just able to see the murder site from the window. What's that bit about second base supposed to mean?"

"'If at first you don't succeed, try second base,'" Greg quoted. "And it so happens I'm glad you're here. I want you to get through to Control and have them rush the staff background checks, and then do a special search. I want a printout of every major theft occurring outside this country in the last three months. By major I mean something that would require a good-size organization to pull off, and I want that list to be *complete*. Tell them I expect to get it before lunchtime tomorrow."

"If anyone in records survives this case, they'll probably come after you when it's over," Anita commented. "Is that it?"

"No," Greg admitted, grinning again. "I also want everything we have on the Morescu, most especially pictures or descriptions of known or suspected members. Since they're involved in this case, the data should already be available."

"I'm seriously impressed," Anita said, her expression more one of delighted surprise. "After so much time we're suddenly beginning to move. If this is what a little smooching with Laine Randall does for you, you'll definitely have to do it more often."

"What did this for me was *arguing* with Laine Randall," he responded with a laugh. "She and I discussed the case, and every time she said, 'But that doesn't make sense,' I knew she was right. We've been looking at this thing from the wrong angle, but I think I've got it turned properly now. And I also understand why she was able to help the police those times. Events around her have to have a certain logic, and if they don't she notices. I've never met anyone like her."

"Then I'm glad she's on our side," Anita said with a smile. "Ah...how did you come to be discussing the case?"

"We started out arguing about whether or not her friend Bob Samson is involved," Greg told her, immediately deciding to leave the blackmail aspect unmentioned. "She refuses to believe he can have anything to do with this, but I'm still not convinced. He happened to be in the middle of a telephone call last night during the first murders, but just because there's an open, connected line to somewhere on your phone, that doesn't mean you're talking. You can be out killing people while the receiver just lies there."

"It sounds like you got to read the statements made to the sheriff's people," Anita observed. "Was there anything else useful in the file?"

"Nothing I can put my finger on right now," Greg said with a distracted shake of his head. "I have the feeling there was *something*, but I'm just not noticing it. Maybe something from tomorrow's reports will help it click into place."

"Tomorrow's reports," Anita echoed, with her brows raised high. "You've already arranged to see them? Greg, you haven't been really taking advantage of Laine Randall, have you? I mean, you haven't done anything that will cause her pain once this is all over?"

"You're worried about *me* taking advantage of Laine Randall?" he asked, then laughed with true amusement. "I flatly refuse to go into details, but it's me you should be worrying about, not her. That lady is absolutely incredible, and if I get out of this with professional reputation intact, it will be a pure miracle. If it gets much worse, I may need you to protect me."

"Me, side with you against another woman?" Anita asked politely, but with a gleam in her eyes. "I love you like a brother, Greg, but if you think I'll protect you, you're out of your mind. You've needed to be taken advantage of for years."

"Ah ha! Then you women do have a club!" Greg accused, pointing a finger at her. "I always knew it, but just lacked the proof. Well, if I have to stand alone against Laine Randall, I'll just have to gather my courage and do it. While *you're* taking care of other matters."

"Yes, sir," Anita answered with a sigh. "And while I'm doing the taking care of, will you be getting your beauty sleep?"

"Sure," he said with another grin. "Right after I do a little more elbow rubbing. The night is still young for those in the casino and Show Room, and I want to look at faces. Unless I'm completely mistaken, there has to be at least one member of Morescu here."

"Then I hope you're mistaken," Anita said, frowning now. "Those people go so far beyond nasty—Greg, you *will* be careful? I'd hate to have to finish this alone."

"I'd hate for you to have to," he answered with a smile. "And Anita—have you made any friends on the staff?"

"A couple of acquaintances," she said with a shrug. "I haven't had much time for socializing, after all. Why do you ask?"

"The two victims tonight were members of the staff," he told her, all amusement gone. "Lundgren was also a member of the staff. If someone gets friendly and invites you out for a moonlight stroll—don't go."

"You really know how to ruin a girl's social life," she said, but Greg could see that she'd paled a bit. "All right, if it means that much to you. And I'll see you tomorrow unless there's a problem or an emergency."

"Tomorrow," he agreed, watching her leave. Once she was gone he knew he should go, too. But he stood in the middle of the room for a moment, thinking private thoughts. Laine was undoubtedly already in bed, and his pulse beat faster at that idea. He wished with everything in him that he could be there beside her, holding her in his arms as he had earlier, kissing her and touching her and ready to give her his love.

But he had business to take care of, and she disliked the thought of accepting him while Robert Amberon prowled elsewhere in the suite. He couldn't blame her for that and certainly didn't, but tomorrow would be another story. In his room there would be no one else around, and she'd already all but agreed. He wasn't sure he could wait that long without breaking, but he would certainly give it his best shot.

And would enjoy every bit of attention she gave him until she turned around and walked away. Some of his happiness faded at the thought of that, but it had happened to him so often he must surely be getting used to it. She would see him exactly for what he was, and then she would go back to her own life and leave him to his. It had always happened that way, and probably always would.

But as Greg turned to leave his room, he knew that this time it would hurt so much more.

Chapter Fifteen

Laine left her suite by going through the hedge wall of the pool area, and only just managed to keep from making enough noise to wake the entire state. She had the feeling Greg had done the same thing a lot more easily, but she couldn't very well have asked him about his methods. If he knew she'd gone out prowling on her own, he would have been very unhappy with her.

"To say the least," she muttered to herself as she slipped from shadow to shadow. She was dressed all in black and had used flattener from her makeup kit to dull her too light complexion. A simple rubber band held her long black hair at the base of her neck, and she wore black driving gloves. If anyone saw her, the last thing they'd believe was that she was out for an innocent stroll.

Which meant she couldn't let anyone see her. The sheriff and his deputies were all over the place, but she deliberately hadn't waited for them to leave. If the guilty were going to be sneaking around—and something told her there was a damned good chance of that—then *they* would be waiting for the police to leave. Laine wanted to be in place already, to see them as they tiptoed by.

And maybe do more than just see them. As she crouched behind a short hedge, her fingers went to the small automatic snugged away in its ankle holster. If she had to she would use the gun, making sure anyone she faced understood that clearly. Anyone mixed up in this was also mixed up in Nissa's murder, and with that in mind *not* pulling the trigger would be the problem. When that truth sank in to whomever was responsible, she might even get some answers.

Deputies were taping around the second murder scene now that the bodies were gone, and Laine couldn't hold back a shudder. She liked to think she understood the murderer mentality, but her understanding was intellectual rather than emotional.

Laine shuddered a second time, then realized how wise she'd been to leave Bob behind. If he'd been there he would have insisted she go back to the suite, and that she refused to do. Besides, he'd had enough problems for one night. She and her automatic could have kept him safe out here, but he'd be safer yet in his own bed.

All she had to do now was wait for the police to leave...

It took more than an hour before the area grew quiet, and during that time Laine had had one scare that had nothing to do with murder. From where she hid she could see the front of her suite, and Sheriff Stoddard had gone over and knocked. Bob had answered the door, left for a moment, then come back to shake his head. The sheriff must have wanted to know if she was still awake, and Bob must have gone to see that her bedroom light was out. If the sheriff had asked Bob to wake her...

But he hadn't, so everything was all right. It couldn't have been anything really important that he wanted to tell her, otherwise he would have had her wakened. The next day she'd be certain to check on the point.

Right then everything was quiet, except for the occasional cart trundling out to take people to their suites. Most of the guests were still inside enjoying themselves, just as though there weren't four people already dead. But maybe they were doing that *because* there were two more bodies, Laine realized. The werewolf had claimed his victims for the night, and now everyone else would be safe.

But was that necessarily true? Movie lore said the werewolf needed to kill every night of the full moon, but unless Laine was mistaken that meant once at least, not *only* once. There was a big difference between the two points, one she was able to appreciate all alone in the silent, cooling dark.

"And one I wish I hadn't thought of," she muttered to herself very low, trying not to begin looking over her shoulder. If someone tried to sneak up on her, she would certainly hear them. And before they could do any sneaking up, they would have to see her. Which they couldn't, not in that inky dark between suites. Empty, silent, inky dark.

I'd better decide right now how long to stay out here, Laine thought as a stray night breeze tickled past her ear. Either someone will turn up quickly, or they won't show until the really wee hours. Do I want to sit down and wait, or—

Her internal debate was cut short by an odd noise that sounded like a scraping half step. She froze where she stood by a hedge, straining her ears for more of the same, but there was nothing. What she could see of the walkway was completely empty, and she could actually see quite a distance down. Nothing and no one, no sight, no sound. Just imagination...

Or maybe not quite. The scraping noise came again, from the dark near a suite farther down the line. Laine felt her ears tingle and the hair at the nape of her neck stir, and then she became aware of the odor...like wet, dirty dog hair...

"There are no such things as werewolves," she whispered soundlessly to herself, but her mouth was dry with fear and her heart had begun to pound. She hadn't been serious about investigating werewolves, hadn't believed there was any such thing, but now in the dark...smelling that odor and hearing that noise...

Hearing it getting closer. Whatever it was or wasn't, it was definitely approaching. Step by scraping half step it was getting nearer, and now Laine could hear faint, occasional panting. It was sneaking its way toward her, and in just a few minutes would be right in her lap. She wasn't all that far from the two previous death scenes; did that thing intend creating a third?

Terror had begun to make her tremble despite the way she was frozen in place, and then something really strange happened. She thought fleetingly about dying not far from the spot where Nissa had been slain, and that *stopped* and *changed* everything. Nissa was *dead,* and chances were that whatever was coming at Laine was responsible!

Rage erupted in flames to burn the terror away, rage at whoever or whatever had so carelessly ended her friend's life.

Laine reached down to her small automatic with a trembling hand, but this time the shaking was caused by anger. If there was any attacking to be done, she was the one who would do it. Right now she wanted blood as badly as any werewolf to pay for the innocence it had spilled. The thing wasn't far away, and in another few steps she would have it.

She began moving toward the end of the hedge, her step soundless, all her attention on what was coming toward her. She still couldn't see anything, but that smell was getting strong enough to be sickening. The thought came that her gun might turn out to be useless, but she was too angry to care. If it came down to it, she was wild enough to use her fingernails.

And then everything seemed to happen at once. Just as she reached the end of the hedge and was about to storm around it, an unearthly howl sounded along with a flurry of footsteps. A shout rang out from somewhere behind her, a few more footsteps, and then she was being knocked to the ground.

She struggled wildly against the weight on her back, trying to free her wrist from the immovable strength of the hand wrapped around it. There was a confusion of other sounds, and then nothing beyond receding footsteps racing away and her own panting breath.

"Laine, let go of the gun!" a voice growled in her ear. "I want to go after that thing, but I don't want you shooting me in the back. Do you hear me?"

"Greg, you idiot, get off me!" she returned, still trying to struggle. "I want to go after it, too!"

"I'll do it for the both of us, while you check out what it threw," he said, and then he was up and racing into the far shadows. Laine surged to her feet, intent on following, and then she realized what Greg had said. Threw? The thing had thrown something?

Laine was reluctant to abandon the thought of giving chase, but in the dark she and Greg would end up shooting each other. The gun in his hand had been very obvious and besides, her curiosity was aroused. Why would a werewolf come sneaking through the dark to *throw* something?

She looked around first to make sure there was no one in sight, then she approached the thing lying on the walk leading to her suite. The faint light from above the door cast shadows over the torn corpse of what seemed to have been a long-eared rabbit. The smell from it was strong where she stood, the pathetic fur wet with its own blood. She'd clearly been sent a message, but one that didn't make any sense.

Laine was deep in thought when the sound of footsteps came, but not so deep that she didn't swing around immediately and bring her gun up. Greg appeared around the end of the hedge, paused until she'd lowered the weapon, then came up to join her.

"It had too much of a lead," he reported disgustedly. "It lost itself in the dark before I could—Laine, what in hell are you *doing* out here?"

"Hunting," she answered shortly, putting away the small automatic. "What were *you* doing? If you hadn't knocked me down I might have had it."

"From where I stood, it looked like it was about to be the other way around," he countered in a hard voice. "It started to charge before it howled, and you would have run right into it. Are you really that determined to get yourself killed?"

"You saw it?" Laine demanded, ignoring the rest of what he'd said. "What did it look like?"

"Through the hedge it looked like a large, black shadow," he answered, almost in a growl. "Don't you ever intend to pay any attention to me?"

"The way you mean it, no," she responded, then looked around. "But I'd like to know why no one else is paying any attention. That howl should have brought out everyone who heard it."

"Not everyone," Greg disagreed, also looking around. "There are a lot of people still at the show or in the casino, and anyone who was back would have enough sense not to investigate. Anyone but you, that is."

"Thanks," she returned dryly. "But since the message was for me, I was supposed to respond. I'd guess that says, 'Back off or you'll end up the same way.' Do you see anything more or less?"

"No," he answered, staring down at the small corpse. "The only thing I don't understand is why they would do it *this* way."

"The same thought occurred to me," she agreed. "There are already four human bodies. If they wanted me to stop, why is the fifth body a rabbit? Why not break into the suite and do it the proper way?"

"Maybe they were afraid you would be too well guarded," Greg suggested. "I came out here to look around and make sure you were all right before I called it a night, and—wait a minute. What about your friend, Amberon? Even if no one else is out here, why isn't *he?*"

"Bob!" Laine breathed, then she was running for the door to the suite, Greg right behind her. That howl had been loud enough and horrible enough to wake anyone, so why hadn't Bob come out to investigate? If they'd done anything to him . . .

Laine tore inside, heading directly for Bob's bedroom as soon as her key card opened the door. Frantic was too mild a word for the way she felt, but she was almost afraid to throw open his door and hit the light switch. She was sick over what she might find.

But there was no blood. Bob lay in the big bed under the covers, snoring softly. Relief flooded over her so strongly that she felt dizzy, but there was still something wrong.

"Bob?" she called, walking closer to put a hand on his shoulder. "Bob, wake up."

"He can't be asleep," Greg said from behind her, reaching out to raise one of Bob's eyelids. "I'll bet you anything he's been drugged. It looks like he had a nightcap with a little something extra in it."

Laine also saw the glass on his bedside table, and picked it up to sniff at its contents. She wasn't good enough to detect the presence of drugs, but she could detect what kind of liquor it was.

"Scotch," she said, putting the glass back. "This means they wanted only him drugged, not me. I don't like Scotch and never drink it."

"This also means they wanted you alone when you found that rabbit," Greg said. "If you'd been in here and heard that howl, you would have gone out. You would have expected Bob to be right behind you, but you would have found yourself alone. It should have been enough to give you second thoughts at the very least."

"Instead, it's giving me third thoughts," she said, refusing to show the shiver she felt. "Shouldn't we call an ambulance for Bob? We can't just leave him lying here."

Rather than answering immediately Greg stepped over to pick up the glass, dunked a finger in it, then tasted a drop of the liquid with the tip of his tongue. Recognition flashed in his eyes, and he put the glass back.

"Standard knockout drops," he told her, rubbing his finger dry with his other hand. "The most a hospital can do is pump his stomach, but it's already gone into his bloodstream. He should wake up in the morning with a headache, but otherwise be perfectly all right."

Laine's hesitation was very brief. "I'll take your word for it. You obviously have experience with these things, and I don't think Bob would appreciate waking up in a hospital bed."

She looked down at her friend's sleeping face one more time, then led the way out of the room and to her own. She'd turned out the light and closed the door, but couldn't quite do the same with her thoughts.

"What's the matter?" Greg asked quietly after watching her take off her gloves and toss them away. "If you'd like to have a doctor confirm what I told you, I won't be insulted. We haven't known each other long enough for you to trust me."

"But I do trust you," she said, turning to look at him where he stood. "If I didn't, I would have pointed out that I missed getting the werewolf because of you. I may be the biggest damned fool alive, but I trust you completely."

"Then what's wrong?" he repeated, the oddest look in his pale, mesmerizing eyes. "If you're not worrying about being alone with me, then what's bothering you?"

"They must have gotten in here after Bob and I left for dinner," she said, beginning to pace around the room. "What if it hadn't been knockout drops in his drink? What if they'd used poison instead? Bob would be dead now instead of just sleeping, and it would be all my fault. They don't want me investigating werewolves."

"Neither do I, but I also won't let you blame yourself," Greg said, and then he was intercepting her in the pacing to pull her into his arms. "Amberon's a big boy now, big enough to not be forced into doing things he doesn't want to. Staying here and helping you was *his* choice, even after they started playing rough. But if you really want to keep him safe, there's only one thing you can do."

"I know," she answered, looking up into his face from the circle of his arms. His broad hands felt so good against her, so strong and supporting. "First thing tomorrow I'm sending Bob home, whether or not he wants to go. Then I can do my investigating with a clear head."

"That's not what I meant," Greg pronounced, looking at her with lowered brows. "I meant you should *stop* investigating, before they shred *you* instead of a rabbit. Don't you have any idea how I'd feel if something happened to you?"

"No, I don't," she answered softly, raising one finger to touch his face. "Why don't you tell me about it?"

She could see the surprise in his eyes, but that was nothing compared to the surprise she felt at herself. She'd never been so straightforward with a man. And a man she barely knew! It probably would have been a lot smarter to suspect him than trust him, but she couldn't seem to do it. She believed everything he told her—and she also believed in him.

"Are you sure?" he asked, the full question unnecessary. "You don't know the whole me yet, and when you do you might regret this. I thought I could simply go along with whatever happened, but somehow you've become too important. I don't want you being hurt by anything, most especially not by me."

"If you're looking for a statement of willingness written in blood, your requirements are at the very least appropriate," she returned with a sigh. "You're also making this very difficult for me. Since I've never before backed a man into a corner, I'm not sure of the proper procedure. Am I supposed to take your clothes off first, or carry you to the bed first? Or doesn't it make a difference?"

"Which comes first is usually a matter of taste," he told her, the grin he wore warming his eyes. "And speaking of taste..."

His lips came down to hers then, tasting rather than kissing. Laine had never felt that often-mentioned tingle from a kiss, but she was certainly feeling it now. Her whole body tingled as she leaned into his, her hands sliding up the muscled hardness of his back. She was under his jacket, but his shirt was still in the way.

"I was only bluffing," she murmured between kisses, an admission that was faintly embarrassing. "I don't have the nerve to take your clothes off, but—"

He silenced her in the most pleasant way possible, but he also slipped out of his jacket one arm at a time. Once it was off he opened his bow tie with a pull, then began on his shirt buttons. Before it was off, though, he ended the kiss and stepped back from her.

"Time out for disarming," he told her in a husky voice. "You can drop a jacket or tie without worrying, but the same doesn't go for a gun. And I really wish you would do the same. Making love to a woman who's armed does unpleasant things to my technique."

"I can't imagine why you'd be intimidated," Laine said with a laugh, her own voice a bit uneven. "Doesn't a small gun make only a small hole?"

"There's no such thing as a small automatic," he answered from behind the back she'd turned to reach down to the ankle holster. "Somehow I have the feeling you already know that."

Laine did know it, which was the reason she carried the weapon. She opened the fasteners and removed both holster and gun, then walked two steps to a table where she put them down.

In all that time she hadn't looked back at Greg, but not because she didn't want to. It was stupid for a woman of experience to be feeling flustered, but she wanted that time with him so badly. *He,* on the other hand, had just about needed to be knocked down and ravished. Maybe he was only pretending willingness to be polite.

"I think it's time for the time-out to be over," his voice murmured from directly behind her, and then two large hands came to slide slowly down her arms. "Or in other words, ready or not, here I come."

Laine couldn't help laughing at the familiar challenge she hadn't heard since childhood. It was so unbelievably fitting for the way she felt when she was with Greg. As lighthearted as a child, safe and protected even though she was playing high on the monkey bars. Feeling that way didn't make sense, not when so many other men had simply let her fall.

He turned her gently toward him before gathering her close again, and her body flared with the awareness that his shirt was gone. She slipped her hands around to his back as his lips took hers again, the feel of his warm, hard body almost enough to make her moan. He held her as if he'd waited half of forever to do it, and now meant to continue on through the other half.

Awareness of everything that wasn't Greg slipped away from Laine, but a short time later it wasn't surprising to find that they were on the bed. He had opened her shirt and was kissing her throat, while his hands were sliding her stretch pants down. At some point she must have kicked off her shoes; her bare toes were rubbing at his leg in response to the presence of his hands.

"I want to feel more of you, Greg," she whispered, her eyes closed against the trembling delight his least touch produced. He could take his own things off before doing the rest of hers.

"Go right ahead," he murmured with a chuckle. "Everything of mine is already off."

Laine didn't believe she could have missed him doing that, but sliding her hands down his lean, powerful hips proved he hadn't lied. Touching him was driving her absolutely insane, especially when she reached his desire. It was no longer possible to doubt his willingness, and hers had never been in doubt.

Almost in a frenzy she got rid of her blouse and bra, then pulled his head up to kiss him. Her body thrust against his in an effort to hurry him, but for that he was totally uncooperative. He caressed her even as he got rid of the rest of her clothes, and kept on touching her. Sounds of deep pleasure came from his throat, which simply added to the deliciousness of his touch.

And he turned out to be right. When he finally moved between her thighs, the frenzy had become a desire for completeness. There was no rushing to get to it and get it over with; he entered her slowly and lovingly, and she received him in the same way. After that they moved together, harder and faster until the frenzy returned, but at that point it was right that it should. It took them both to the heart of a sun, bathed them in its heat, pushed them to the flare of explosion.

Afterward there was a sense of satisfaction she had never before experienced, which turned her world even brighter when Greg kissed her deeply before withdrawing. It was over and yet it wasn't, a contradiction Laine hadn't the strength to understand. All she wanted to think about was the extreme pleasure just past, pleasure that had somehow gone beyond the physical.

Greg collapsed on the bed beside the woman he had just made love to, silently cursing himself in the vilest terms. He'd just had the time of his life, an experience that had satisfied both mind and body. He wanted it to be the first time of many, but the odds were so completely against him. How many times had it started out great, only to fall away in ashes?

And this time it had been more than great, even better than he'd thought it could be. What would he do when she turned around and hurried away? He'd started missing her even before this; what would he do *now?* Carry the pain with him for the rest of his days?

He was certain that none of his thoughts had reached his face, but when he turned his head to the left she was staring at him. Propped up on an elbow, her soft black hair flowing over one shoulder, she studied his face in a way that confused him. The look in those green eyes was unrecognizable, and reluctant or not he just had to ask.

"Is something wrong?" His hand rose to her back with the words, taking the opportunity to stroke her satin skin. If that turned out to be the last time he could touch her...

"I was just wishing you weren't so damned handsome," she answered with a sigh, bringing one hand up to touch his face with a finger. "Couldn't you *try* to be uglier?"

"I'm not sure I want to know what you're talking about," he ventured, wondering if he looked as wide-eyed as he felt. "I mean, what happens if you explain it and I understand you? Now, there's a scary thought."

"Stop teasing me," she protested, leaning forward to rest her cheek against his chest. "You know damned well I can't explain what I mean. How soon will you be leaving?"

"I'd been thinking about second or third thing in the morning," he answered, now stroking her tousled hair. "Is this your way of telling me I'd better think again?"

"You'll stay the night?" she asked in surprise, sitting up fast to look at him again. Then the surprise faded. "Oh. Of course you're staying. Bob is dead to the world, and you don't want me going out hunting again. Well, you don't have to worry. I'm in for the night."

"I'm glad to hear that," he said. "I'd hate having to get up again for anything but a shower. You don't mind if I use your shower? You can stand guard while I'm in there, and then I'll do the same for you."

"So that's it," she said flatly. "You're after me for my bathroom. You rent a cheap room in the hotel itself, then find some unsuspecting woman in a suite to romance. Once you're in her bed, you have her bathroom as well. The oldest con story in the world, and *I* fell for it."

She stared at him with bitter self-mockery, for all the world like a woman betrayed, and Greg simply didn't understand.

"What in hell are you talking about?" he demanded as he sat up, totally bewildered. "Laine, what did I do? I can see you're hurt, but I don't know what I did."

"You took first dibs on the shower," she answered with a sudden grin that wiped away everything else. "Now you should be feeling guilty enough to let *me* go first. You don't mind, do you?"

She leaned forward to brush her lips across his with the question, and Greg had the definite urge to close his eyes. She'd looked so seriously upset that he hadn't listened to what she was *saying,* and she'd caught him with a really bad joke. To have a woman accuse him of being after her for her *bathroom...*

"Don't you know it's cheating for you to do that?" he asked darkly. "You looked like you meant every word you said, and I was feeling like the biggest heel ever born. It so happens I have *never* chased a woman for her bathroom. Maybe a pantry or two when I was young, but I do have my principles."

"Oooh, I knew you were a man of principle," she came back with the most delightful laugh, those beautiful green eyes shining. "I'm a woman of interest, so I have an instinct about these things. Would you really mind? About the shower, I mean."

"I'm open to persuasion," he allowed, keeping his grin to a modest leer. "I think you *owe* me a little persuasion after that act, making me feel so awful . . . as if no one in the whole world loved me."

"Oh, poor baby!" She was instantly contrite, moving closer to slip her arms under his.

His own arms had already closed around her. She was the craziest woman he had ever met, and matching her craziness was something he wanted to do forever. He didn't know if all actresses were like her, but the fact was he didn't care. *She* was all that mattered, and he tasted her mouth deeply as his hands began to move over her again.

She did end up taking the first shower, but not for quite some time.

LAINE FELT THE DARKNESS all around her, but seeing into it was completely impossible. She could hear night sounds, smell something like fog and taste the edge of fear, but she couldn't see. The darkness had secrets it meant to keep, even as it kept its hold on her.

But there were others out there in the dark, others who couldn't see her because she wore black. They weren't using anything but eyesight, and might not even know she was there. But she knew about *them*, and she also knew who they were. Bob was one, and he was searching for her frantically. He knew *the other* was there as well, and he was frightened for her.

And well he might be. Laine heard the scraping half-step of *the other,* knowing how close it was. It hadn't spilled her blood yet, but if she stumbled into contact with it, it would. She was moving and it was moving, and sooner or later they would meet.

Fear flooded through her body at the thought, a terrible paralyzing fear that turned her arms and legs to lead. She wanted very much to find somewhere safe to hide, but something refused to let her stop moving through the dark. There was a debt she owed, one that had to be repaid no matter how terrified she was. She was a good enough actress to fool even herself into believing the fear wasn't there, but—

Laine froze, only the trembling in her bones and the clang of her heart continuing on. *The other* was very near, so close that it would soon find out how frightened she was. She had to get moving again to prevent that, had to find *him* where he searched the dark on his own. *He* would help her, stand with her, protect her . . .

And then a hand reached out of the nothingness to close on her shoulder. She wanted to scream at that blood-dampened touch and then she *was* screaming, helpless to keep the terror inside. Wildly she threw herself around, trying to remember what to do to protect herself . . .

"Laine, it's all right," a voice said, sounding as though it had said the same thing over and over. "Wake up, love. I'm here and it's all right. I won't let anyone hurt you."

Strong hands kept her from doing any damage until she understood that it had been a dream. Then he pulled her close to hold her to a broad body that was warm and comforting. A dream, it had only been a bad dream. Laine's heart raced and her inner self trembled.

But *he* had found her, even through all that darkness. She'd hoped he would, because she trusted him. He'd never be like the others, urging her to lean on him and then stepping away. *He* would never let her fall, never just be using her. She held to him as he stroked her hair, feeling safe and happy.

Her eyes closed as she began to drift off again, no more than the tiniest doubt floating in her mind.

Chapter Sixteen

Laine sat drinking coffee on her patio the next morning, her thoughts marching blindly in five directions. She had never before in her life felt scatterbrained, but that morning was making it happen. For such a pretty morning, that was a dirty trick to pull.

Greg had been wonderfully obliging earlier when she'd awakened him with a kiss, and then they'd shared breakfast on that very same patio. By the time they were through Bob was beginning to show signs of coming around, so Greg had kissed her one last time and left.

But not before ordering her to stop investigating werewolves. The nightmare she'd had really bothered him, possibly even more than it did her. That was why he'd given her those flat-voiced orders; he was determined to keep her safe by getting her uninvolved. But even assuming she *wanted* out, how did you uninvolve yourself from a mess like that? It simply wasn't possible, and if Greg wasn't so personally involved he would have seen that for himself.

Which was why she wasn't bothered by his trying to order her around. He thought he was doing it for her, and hadn't yet learned that Laine paid very little attention to orders. She was used to making up her own mind about things, so people giving her orders were only wasting their breath.

"I've arranged to get a room in the main building," Bob said as he joined her at the table, reaching for his own coffee cup. "You're not the only one in the world who can play stubborn."

"You'd rather play dead?" Laine asked, furious with him but refusing to show it. "Why can't you be reasonable and go home? You're not proving what you think you are, you know. All you're doing is distracting me."

"And what is it you think I'm trying to prove?" he demanded, but gently out of deference to his still-aching head. "That I can be just as loyal to a friend as you are? That I refuse to keep myself safe at the expense of someone I care a lot about? If you can do it, what makes it so wrong for me? And when I pay attention, I can damned well take care of myself. Let me stay here."

"No way in hell," Laine said as flatly as she had ever said anything. "If I get you out of the line of fire, you'll be *able* to pay attention. To something besides me, at least. I—"

Her words were cut short by the sound of the doorbell, the first time she'd heard it in the suite. Rather than continue an argument with a stubborn mule, she left the table and went to answer it. Outside the door was a deputy holding a folder, and he took his hat off as soon as he saw Laine.

"Mornin', ma'am," he said to her. "The sheriff sent this over for you, an' he said to say he hopes it does some good. He also said to ask if you're gettin' anywhere with what you're doin'."

"Last night the answer would have been no," Laine said, opening the folder to see two autopsy reports. "As of very early this morning, it changed to a most definite maybe. Why are there reports on the latest killings, but still none on my friend Nissa?"

"Things started gettin' backed up," the deputy said with an apologetic gesture. "The new coroner was goin' too slow, so the sheriff asked old Doc to come in an' help out. Right now they're both workin' on your friend. By this afternoon they oughta be all caught up."

"About time," Laine muttered, noticing that there was a different, shakier signature at the bottom of the reports. "Not that I expect it to be of help. Nothing seems to be helping here."

"You can say that again," the deputy agreed fervently. "We don't find much, no more 'n a couple of hairs or a print, an' then can't even use it. County prosecutor near blew up when the sheriff told him what we had, an'—Well, it wasn't good."

Laine could imagine. If it had been her job to take a case into court, she wouldn't have wanted to hear that the only solid evidence available was wolf hairs and paw prints—from something other than a normal wild animal.

"I'm sure it won't do any good, but I also have something for you," she told the deputy. "Do you see the body of that rabbit, over there near the hedge? Well, someone threw it at my suite last night, in what I'm sure was an effort to frighten me. You might have your pathologists check it over, to see if that someone got careless and left a clue we *can* use. If the sheriff wants more details about the incident, just have him call me. There isn't much, but it's his if he wants it."

The deputy nodded in a preoccupied way, his attention mostly on the small corpse Laine had had Greg shift out of clear sight. Since their conversation was over, Laine left him to his unpleasant chore and went back inside the suite. Bob was still at the table on the patio, but when he saw her he finished his coffee and rose.

"That file tells me I'd be wasting my time trying to talk sense into you," he observed, his tone neutral. "You're going on with this no matter what anyone says or does. What will you do if you need me and I'm not here?"

"I'll do a hell of a lot better than if I needed you and you were dead," Laine returned flatly. "I've already lost one friend to this thing. I'm not about to lose another. I want you to stay out of it, Bob, and I'm not joking."

"If I don't, will you dock my pay?" he asked with a snort. "If so, then you'd better start docking. As soon as I get rid of this headache, you'll be finding yourself with a second shadow. *I'm* not ready to lose any more friends, either."

With that he strode back into the suite, probably to move his things to the separate room he'd reserved. Laine would have preferred seeing him leave the resort entirely, but having him away from her might be nearly as good. After what had happened she almost wondered why he *wasn't* leaving, but the answer was obvious. She was still his Chinese Obligation.

Sitting down at the table, Laine freshened her coffee from the carafe, then opened the file she'd been sent. It was obvious the sheriff hadn't gotten anything useful from the autopsy results, but maybe she'd have better luck. He'd probably sent her the file with just that hope in mind. Once she looked it over, she'd take it to Greg's room and trade it for his files. There had to be something *somewhere*.

UNDER OTHER CIRCUMSTANCES, Greg might have felt conspicuous crossing a lobby in the middle of the morning while still wearing evening clothes. Right now he was too distracted to care. One of the things distracting him was the night and morning just past, and the way Laine had smiled when he'd laid down the law. He didn't want her to continue putting herself in danger, but she wasn't going to be listening to him.

"And I used to think I liked the idea of independent women," he growled to himself, punching the elevator button for his floor with more strength than necessary. "I should have had my head examined."

The smoothly closing elevator doors made no comment to that, which was lucky for Greg's frame of mind. He knew he was still partial to independent women, but anyone pointing that out would have had a fight on their hands.

"I've got to get this thing settled fast, or one of us won't survive it," he muttered, glad there was no one else there to hear him talking to himself again. That woman was able to set him talking to himself without the least effort, so when she made the effort it was a good deal harder on him.

The elevator dinged as the doors opened on his floor, which was another good thing. If it hadn't he might have ridden it down again, lost in thought about how incredible his time with Laine had been. And *she* seemed to have enjoyed it as well. Was there even the least chance that things would end differently this time?

"Sure," he breathed, walking slowly down the hall to his room. About as much chance as having this case wrap itself up in the next hour. He was already lost where Laine Randall was concerned, but the feeling wasn't likely to be mutual.

Depression added itself to his mood as he carded into his room, flipping on the light switch as he passed it. The dossiers he'd asked for on the staff would help in distracting him, so he hoped they'd already arrived. Anita would have been able to—

The sound of a footstep behind him gave him no more than an instant's warning, but Greg's trained reflexes made that instant count. His left hand came up even as the cord whipped around his throat in preparation for tightening, and he was able to get his fingers between the knot and his windpipe before it did. With that done he could bring his right elbow back hard into the ribs of whomever stood behind him, his most immediate intention a more permanent loosening of the cord.

Greg heard a low grunt in a male voice as his elbow connected, but it took two more blows of the same sort before the cord was dropped. He pulled loose and moved forward before turning fast, knowing he wasn't about to face someone who would be easy to take. At the very least he'd cracked one of his attacker's ribs, but the man hadn't gone down moaning and writhing.

In point of fact, the man looked like he hadn't even noticed being hurt. He stood at least as tall as Greg, with dark hair and eyes and the expressionless face of a professional assassin. His clothes and gloves were all nondescript and dark, nothing that would cause anyone to remember seeing him. The garrote he'd tried using had been thrown to one side, and his left hand was now wrapped around the hilt of a wide-bladed knife.

Greg remembered the automatic holstered at the small of his back, but made no attempt to draw it. The problem with that big a gun was that it was too easy to kill someone without meaning to, and Greg didn't want his attacker dead. This man was no street tough; he would know who had hired him, and could also be made to talk. Greg knew some very effective ways, even if they weren't recognized in a court of law.

But first he would have to make the man his prisoner, preferably without getting sliced to strips in the process. He was already standing defensively, knees slightly bent and fists raised, right side toward his attacker. Guarding against a left side attack was awkward for a right-handed fighter, but hopefully it would be even worse for the man if he wasn't naturally left-handed.

Which he wasn't. His cracked rib was on the right side, so the man was using his left hand in an attempt to finish what he'd started. But he wasn't ungainly to the point of clumsiness. Greg kicked twice, lightning fast, trying to send the knife flying from the man's hand, but neither kick worked. The man avoided them with difficulty.

And then, without warning, the man screamed and threw himself at Greg, the knife blade held flat and ready to plunge into flesh. Greg's body reacted without thought, his right arm blocking the knife blow, his left fist driving hard to the middle of his attacker's body. It was a one-two meant to end the fight then and there, and it did. The stranger dropped his knife, and folded to the floor.

But not just to lie there. The man began gasping and convulsing, his impassive face darkening, his hands clawing at his throat. Greg cursed and went down to one knee, knowing the man wasn't faking, but there was nothing he could do. Even as he reached out, his former attacker convulsed one last time and then lay still.

Chapter Seventeen

"I don't believe this," Greg muttered. The man's throat pulse was no longer there. Greg made very sure of that before straightening again. Then he stood staring down at the thug for a moment before going to the phone.

The sheriff's office said the sheriff was right there at the hotel, and agreed to radio through to him and send him to Greg's room. They weren't happy about doing it without a specific reason, but with all the trouble going on they didn't argue long.

Greg had enough time to find the dossiers he'd asked for, sitting on the table where the previous files had been. He'd just put them in a dresser drawer out of sight when the knock came at his door, and he went to answer it hoping it was the sheriff. It was, and when Stoddard stepped inside, Greg quickly closed the door behind him.

"I'm glad to see your people don't drag their feet, Sheriff," he said. "It wasn't my intention to add to your troubles, but I'm afraid I have."

"Does it have anything to do with the reason your arm is bleeding?" Stoddard asked, gesturing toward

Greg's right arm. "If you're going to tell me you need a rabies shot, I don't want to hear it."

"Believe it or not, I was almost that close," Greg said with a small laugh. "But that's another story I'll be telling you later. The first one you have to hear does have to do with this scratch on my arm. The guy who made it is in there."

Stoddard's brows rose when Greg nodded toward the living area, but he walked ahead until the wall that formed the room's entryway no longer blocked sight of the body. Wordlessly he crouched to check the man's pulse the way Greg had, then straightened to look at his host.

"Another dead body was exactly what I needed," he said, his dark eyes more weary than suspicious. "What happened?"

"As soon as I walked in here he came for me with a garrote," Greg answered, pointing out the cord. "When that didn't work he pulled a knife, probably to finish the job quietly. I decided I wanted him saved for questioning, so I didn't use anything but my hands. You can see how well that worked out."

"You're not good enough to avoid accidents like that?" Stoddard asked, and now there was suspicion in his eyes. "If you wanted him alive, he ought to be alive."

"I have an idea," Greg responded with a sigh. "I broke at least one of his ribs getting free of that cord, and then I used a hand blow to put him down. I think that second blow caused the broken rib to pierce his lung, or maybe even his heart. The autopsy will tell us for certain."

"He'll have to take a number," Stoddard muttered with a glance at the corpse. "Make sure you don't disappear until that number comes up. Now, what was that you said earlier about almost being close enough to need a rabies shot?''

"Last night Laine Randall had an unexpected caller," Greg responded, then told Stoddard the story. "If I could have gotten after that thing just a little sooner, I might not have lost it in the dark," he concluded. "Laine claims she hasn't heard anything worth repeating, but that may not be so. She may have been told something she doesn't realize is important, or she may be saving what she knows for her own use. Whichever it is, she refuses to be scared off."

"Do you think that thing saw you when you chased it last night?" Stoddard asked with a frown. "If it did and thinks you may have seen *it,* that could be the reason you have a body on your carpeting—to make sure you don't pass on whatever you might know."

"That idea occurred to me," Greg agreed with a nod. "It's the only possibility that fits, but not all the way. If this has to do with whatever I chased last night, why did a pro come to take care of it? Is there a closer connection than I thought between your murders and the reason I'm here? But that's too bizarre. How can there be?"

"You're asking me?" Stoddard said with a snort. "I'm still trying to figure out why I traded nice, normal urban crime for *this.* And let's not forget I don't yet *know* the reason you're here. It won't be long before I start asking, but right now I'm remembering a request not to interfere. If I hadn't gotten that call, you'd be on your way back to the station with me. Where's your phone?"

Greg pointed it out without comment, but couldn't help reflecting that his people seemed to have made up for not supplying him with the proper background. The sheriff had been soothed with an official call, but one that hadn't told him any more than Greg had. It had bought him some time—not to mention kept him from getting arrested—and he'd have to remember to pass on his thanks.

While the sheriff waited for his people to come and collect the body, Greg jumped in the shower then dressed in clean clothes. The gash on his arm was superficial, little more than a scratch most likely gotten when he was blocking the knife thrust. He came out of the bathroom in time to see his erstwhile attacker being taken away in a body bag, but that wasn't all. The sheriff had already left, but his place had been taken by Laine Randall.

"Greg, what happened?" she demanded as soon as she saw him. "Are you all right?"

"They think I'll live, but I'm not so sure," he answered, delighted to see what looked like worry in her beautiful green eyes. If he got really lucky and it *was* worry... "As soon as we're alone, I'll tell you what I need to guarantee my survival."

"Idiot," she commented, her cheeks coloring very slightly due to the grins of the morgue men. As soon as the door closed behind them, she demanded, "Tell me what happened!"

He sighed and told her, and by the time he was through she was frowning. She was also shaking her head very slightly, as though refusing to accept what she'd heard. Greg had a sudden vision of other women hearing similar things, stories that had turned them pale and unaccepting. A cold knot formed in the pit of his stomach as he cursed the looseness of his tongue, but Laine's first words weren't what he'd been afraid they'd be.

"As soon as we get a bandage on that cut, we'll have to talk about this," she said, her expression troubled. "Considering our previous guesswork, it makes no sense at all. What could you have possibly seen that would justify trying to murder you?"

"Maybe I'm just in the way," he suggested, wishing she would look at something other than him for a while. With those unbelievable eyes staring straight at him, all his thinking ended him up in a place that had nothing to do with the murders.

"I see your point," she agreed with a nod. "They drug Bob so I'll be all alone, and therefore ripe for terrorizing. That's when they try to scare me off, but there *you* are, getting in the way by helping me. I see it, but I don't agree. Where are your bandages?"

"You make it sound like I travel prepared to be hurt," he objected, doing some looking away of his own. She was switching subjects too fast for his current condition, which wasn't far removed from being hit in the head with a bat. It wasn't a bat he'd been hit with, but Laine Randall didn't need props. She was turning out to be deadly to his concentration, and he'd damned well better pull himself together.

"Stop stalling," she ordered, tapping one tennis shoe-clad foot. "I want bandages and some sort of antiseptic, and if you don't come up with them I'll call guest assistance. Would you rather have me taking care of you, or a doctor?"

"I'll get the bandages," he surrendered with another sigh, shaking his head as he went toward his closet. "We're going to have to do something to break you of the blackmail habit. It's usually considered even more harmful to good health than smoking.''

"But I only blackmail people bigger than me," she said with a grin, stepping forward to take his medical kit. "I've always considered it more ladylike than knocking them down and jumping on their heads."

"You could be right," he allowed, loving her devilish look when she grinned. "Is that the file with the latest on the murder victims you're holding? Let me see it."

"First the arm, then we trade," she stated, putting the file aside to open the kit. "Sit down and try not to yell for your mommy."

Greg didn't quite like the sound of that, but he sat down and let her take care of his arm. To his surprise she was exquisitely gentle but briskly efficient, doing the job quickly and without a fuss. He wanted to ask where she'd learned to be that good with bandages, but she was still too deep in the case.

"I think you'll be very surprised when you read the two new autopsy reports," she said as she put away the ointment and bandage roll. "I won't tell you why, because I want to see if you spot the same thing I did. Where are your reports?"

He got the two stacks of dossiers from their separate hiding places, and plunked them down on the table for her. Then he deliberately picked up the autopsy report and took it to a couch, his stare daring her to try to stop him. All she did was grin and start looking through dossiers, so he crossed his legs and began reading.

Nothing but an occasional rattle of paper broke the silence for a while, and once Greg began reading he found himself immediately absorbed. He had to finish the second report before he understood Laine's previous comment, and then he sat back feeling undecided.

"I'll grant you this is strange, but what makes you think it's significant?" he asked with a wave of the folder when Laine looked at him. "Isn't it possible it's just some ghastly coincidence?"

"Have you ever heard the saying that there's no such thing as coincidence?" she countered. "Two people are killed together, and an autopsy shows they were both suffering with terminal illnesses. Come on, Greg. If that isn't significant I don't know what is, but let's talk about this list. Whose list of possessions is it?"

"That's Lundgren's stuff, the man who was killed with your friend," Greg answered. "What about the list?"

"It's all wrong," she said, getting up to hand it to him. "I might have missed the point if I hadn't seen your medical kit. Do you usually have that kit with you?"

"Usually," he agreed cautiously, wondering where she was heading. "More often than not it goes unused, but I usually have it."

"And you would probably still carry it even to a place you thought you might not leave again," she said. "Since there was no guarantee you would die, you'd take the chance you might live."

"And how do you see the list fitting in with that?" he asked with a frown, his mind suddenly going in an odd direction. "You can't mean—"

"That Lundgren wasn't prepared to live." she finished when he didn't. "I certainly do. Take a look at that thing, and tell me why a man would carry an almost empty tube of toothpaste, with no handy replacement. Maybe he meant to get more or change brands when he got here, but the same is true of his shaving cream, after-shave and shampoo. And look at that list of clothing.''

"Nothing new, nothing particularly good, only a single suit," Greg summed up aloud. "No more than an adequate amount of underwear in average condition. No books, personal papers or pictures. Nothing anyone would worry about losing.''

"Exactly," Laine agreed with satisfaction. "And if he meant to buy things here, where's all the money to do it? Was he counting on using his salary? If so, why didn't he use some of the money he did have to start replacing essentials? The first report the sheriff gave me said he had a couple of hundred dollars on him. That's not enough for a new tube of toothpaste?''

"But you're forgetting something," Greg pointed out, his frown so heavy he could feel it. "Lundgren's autopsy didn't show anything terminal, only the second set of victims' did. We're proving a point that isn't even a supposition.''

"And you're proving how important it is to listen to casual comments," Laine told him with even more satisfaction. "I picked up the fact that the medical examiner here is new, which means he's basically inexperienced. He must have been so rattled by the grisliness of the first deaths, he didn't do a thorough job. He was taking so long with the postmortems, in fact, that they brought the old ME out of retirement to help him. He's the one who wrote *these* reports.''

"Which means we need to have him look at Lundgren's body," Greg said, nodding distractedly. "The way he described the death wounds as a shredding of the skin and flesh with sharply pointed objects shows he isn't squeamish, so he ought to do a thorough job. Now all *we* have to do is realign our theories."

"Which won't be nearly as easy," Laine granted with a sigh. "We have two—probably three—dying people who are now dead, at least one of whom was connected somehow with terrorists. Why would terrorists use dying people? So there's no loss if they happen to get caught? Maybe the terrorists didn't know the people were dying."

"I'm willing to bet they did know," Greg said slowly, a coldness creeping inside him. "Lundgren will match the other two, and they'll have known about all three. All of them were sent by the Morescu for a specific purpose, which *must* revolve around the fact that they were dying. We couldn't catch Lundgren smuggling, because it was himself he brought in."

"For what conceivable reason?" Laine demanded, now showing exasperation. "You said there was a lot of money involved, and the Morescu was selling something. Who would want to buy dying people?"

"Haven't you ever heard of death videos?" Greg asked as gently as he could, trying to keep from shocking her too badly. "People are actually killed in them, and other people pay fortunes to get copies. If a man or woman knew they were dying and the family they were leaving behind had no money, they might consider hurrying that death if their families got paid enough. I'm not saying that's the reason, but it all fits."

Laine's fair skin went paler yet, and she left her chair at the table to hurry over to his couch. He took her quickly into his arms and held her tightly to him, feeling the way she was trying not to shiver. Greg realized then that she rarely allowed her true emotions to show, but that didn't mean she wasn't feeling them.

"I was sick the first time I heard about that," she admitted while he stroked her hair. "The whole point of acting is to show real situations without anyone getting hurt. Isn't there enough of death in actual life to satisfy people? It's so twisted—but I still don't agree with you. They can't have come here to be the victims in death videos."

"Why not?" he asked, helpless to ignore how good holding her felt. "The one they're coming to meet gets them jobs here, supplying a reason for bringing them into the country. Once here they quit together, leave with their contact, and no one ever sees them again. Either something went wrong this time, or the videos have already been done."

"You're forgetting one very important question, Greg," she said, shifting just far enough to be able to see him. "Why would the people making the videos need to deal with the Morescu? Usually they choose someone almost at random, then tape the chase and the kill. If they decided to arrange willing victims instead, why would they need to import the people, let alone deal with a very dangerous group? Don't you think there are dying people in need of money in *this* country?"

"I hate women who are so logical," Greg grumbled, pretending to scowl at her. "You're supposed to gush over how brilliant my theories are, not pick them to pieces. So where does that leave us?"

"Out in left field facing a lineup of golfers," she answered with a faint smile. "I think I agree that the Morescu sent those three people here *because* they were dying and not in spite of it, but I haven't a clue as to why. Are we safe in assuming they were supposed to end up dead rather quickly, or is that reaching?''

"As long as we actually have something to reach for, let's go for it,'' Greg said, getting an idea. "If we find it doesn't fit later on, we can toss it out then. Right now I want to see that list of hotel employees. It might help to know how long the second two victims have been here.''

Laine went to get the printout, and brought it back to the couch. Checking the man and woman by name was simple, and the answer they got was interesting.

"They got here only two days before Lundgren,'' Greg said, stating the obvious. "They came separately from two different places, but they arrived at the same time. I wish it was possible to find out if there are any more in their group. If there are, I'd be willing to assume that the deaths were planned and expected.''

"How does that follow?'' Laine asked with raised brows. "And why would it be so hard to find out if other employees arrived only recently?''

"Laine, this is a very large hotel out in the boondocks that boasts about its international cuisine,'' he explained. "They bring people in from all over the world to staff their kitchens, but the people who eat the food are very rich. If they like what they get, they aren't above hiring away certain members of the staff for their own households. And since this place is out in the wilds, there's a large turnover due to boredom. New people are always being hired and arriving, so how do we tell the ones we want from the ones we don't?''

"Waiting for them to become corpses would defeat our purpose,'' she agreed glumly. "But why would the deaths be planned if there were others in the—oh, I think I see. If the deaths *weren't* planned and expected, any other member of the group would be frantic. They might even go to the sheriff for protection."

"Or try to leave," Greg amended with approval. "The only ones being allowed to leave these days are people who were scheduled to leave, and even they have to prove beyond doubt that they can be found again if necessary. So for argument's sake, let's assume the murders were scheduled and expected. *Why* were they scheduled, and what's expected?"

"And how could it make the Morescu a whole lot of money?" Laine added. "I suppose it's possible they're dealing with real werewolves who want to make sure their victims can't be traced back to them. But in that case, why make it so clear the murders were done by a werewolf? Isn't that the least bit self-defeating?"

"It should mean the murders were done by any group *but* werewolves," Greg answered, facing the question soberly. "Vampires, say, would tear up the victims to hide their teeth marks, as well as to throw the blame on werewolves. Ghouls would be trying especially hard to change their familiar MO, and—"

"And none of that explains why they're trying to stop me from investigating," she interrupted, making a face over his irreverence. "We agree werewolves are most likely being framed. If so, why would the framers want me to stop pushing the theory *they* set up? I'm not saying it couldn't be werewolves, I'm trying to prove it was."

"But what if you happen to prove the exact opposite?" Greg suggested. "Then you've blown their whole scam. And don't forget they might only be pretending they want you to stop. If they have any idea about what you're like, they know you'll go on trying to prove exactly what they want you to."

"I don't like the idea of being manipulated into doing their dirty work," she said with what Greg saw was a very attractive frown. "The fact that they haven't hurt me supports what you just said, but it still doesn't feel right. If it had been almost any other woman in my place, what they did would have worked."

"So either they know you very, very well and want you to continue on, or they don't know you at all and want you to stop. Why don't we toss a coin to decide on which."

Greg knew his impatience was showing through, but the whole thing was so frustrating! They'd just discovered something they knew was significant, and still couldn't make head or tail of it.

"Well, whichever way *they* want it, *I* want to conduct one more interview," Laine said, reaching up to run a finger around his ear. "That girl, Sassy, who was one of the two who found the first victims. She claims to have seen something, and I want to hear firsthand what it was. Maybe it will turn out to be a missing puzzle piece."

"Unlikely," Greg commented, but his mind was now forcibly involved with the woman who touched him so lightly. He'd always had a sense of duty that was easily stronger than any possible distraction; now he was beginning to believe that was only because he hadn't yet met Laine Randall.

"And what did you make of the other oddities in the autopsy reports?" she asked from what seemed like a long distance off. "I don't know enough about medical things to understand if we should pay attention to them. What's 'masked incisional evidence,' or 'traces of tissue trauma due to slight incendiary manifestation'?''

"Masked incisional evidence means a scar from surgery that's covered up somehow," he answered automatically. "Vain or professional women have that done to keep the scar from showing. Tissue trauma due to slight incendiary manifestation—that would be tissue burns on the inside, I think, but not a lot of it. Just enough for the ME to notice."

"But where could *that* possibly fit in?" she asked with brows raised. "Hiding surgery scars and being burned on the inside?"

"Your guess is as good as mine," he murmured, beginning to ease her down flat on the couch. "We'll check later with the ME to find out, but if it was important he would have brought it to the sheriff's attention. How do you feel about prelunch quickies?"

"I don't know," she said with a grin, reaching up to put her arms around his neck. "I have to watch my weight, so I've never had one. How do they taste? Lots of calories with whipped cream on top?"

"No, no, no," he corrected with a grin of his own. "That's after-dinner dalliance. Prelunch quickies come without the whipped cream."

"Mmm, sounds delicious," she agreed, already tasting his lips as he began to kiss her. "Why don't we share one, just in case I find I don't like it."

"If you don't like it, I'll give you your money back," he promised, and then lost interest in all banter. Her hands were moving over him just as his were on her. If she turned out not to like it, he'd quit Interpol and enter a monastery.

Chapter Eighteen

Laine chuckled as she entered Greg's bathroom to fix her hair and makeup. His "quickie" had been anything but that, and afterward he'd told her his thought about a monastery. She'd assured him his original career choice was safe, and it certainly was. Every time she shared love with him, it made her want to do it again and again and again.

Which was a hell of an assumption to make. She sighed as she stared at herself in the mirror, knowing she was already in far too deep. Like a silly schoolgirl she had fallen in love with Greg Williams, but there was no guarantee he felt the same. It was much more likely he was just being accommodating while they worked together, and once the mystery was solved . . .

"He'll kiss you goodbye and go back to his own life," she whispered to the reflection filled with misery that stared back at her from the mirror. "He'd hate being married to an actress, especially one who wants to do movies. You'd hardly ever be there for him—assuming he has any real interest in you. Your being beautiful isn't important to him. With his looks, he probably knows enough beautiful women to start his own football team. Offense *and* defense."

And for the first time in her life she wished that wasn't so. She'd met a man she wanted for herself; by now she had the right to ask him about his feelings, but she was terrified at what his answer might be. If she had the choice, she'd rather be attacked by that werewolf than ask. It was possible to defend yourself from a werewolf, but what did you do to fight off heartbreaking disappointment?

"And the old-timers thought they knew the meaning of 'a fate worse than death'," she muttered, quickly running a brush through her hair. "When you find you'd rather be attacked than answered, it's safe to say you have a problem."

But it was a problem she would have to face sooner or later, so did it make sense to put it off? The more she was with Greg, the more she wanted him. Waiting would just make losing him that much harder, and it was already too painful to think about. If she jumped in fast with both feet...the shock passed more quickly that way.

Laine actually felt sick to her stomach, but she had to know. There had already been so many disappointments that her reservoir of hope was running dry. Emptying it entirely would do no one any good. She turned from the mirror and walked to the bathroom doorway, parting her lips to call Greg.

But someone else spoke first. In the mirrored wall across from and to the right of the bathroom, Laine could see the sudden entrance of a woman. She was beautiful in the classic way despite the housekeeping uniform, and she came in with her own card key.

"And where were *you* all night?" she demanded as soon as she saw Greg, exasperation thick in her voice. "Do you have any idea how long I waited? If you

think I'm going to make appointments just to get to
see you—''

And then Greg was beside her, speaking quietly as
he turned her around with one arm and headed her
back toward the door. His words were too soft for
Laine to hear, but his manner with the woman
couldn't be missed. He spoke to her as though she
meant something to him, as though he were charm-
ingly asking her to forgive him. The arm around her
shoulders wasn't the least hesitant, and the warmth in
his smile was horribly obvious.

And the woman was listening. Very slowly her
frown was replaced with a smile, and then she nodded as she reached for the door. She had clearly agreed
to come back later, when Greg would be able to give
her the attention she deserved.

Laine walked slowly back to the bathroom mirror,
this time staring at a woman who felt like a fool. She'd
been so worried about questioning Greg—but getting
the answers hadn't been difficult at all. He *was* just
being accommodating, and once they no longer had a
common aim, that would be the end of it.

"But why doesn't that make a difference?" she
asked her reflection in a whisper. "Since I know that,
why can't I stop loving him?"

Her reflection didn't have an answer, either; it was
too busy trying to blink back tears of pain, a condition that made everything blurry. She'd assumed—
hoped—he cared as much as she did, but it wasn't so.
Now she had to live with that.

Laine washed her face and reapplied the small
amount of makeup she wore off-camera, and by then
she was ready. The hurt she felt would probably never
fade entirely, but it would also never be seen by any-

one. She was a professional, after all, and because of that could spare Greg the embarrassment of needing to say an awkward goodbye. *She* was the one with the problem, so she would deal with it alone.

The smile her reflection wore looked perfectly normal, so she left the bathroom to rejoin the man to whom she was nothing more than an associate.

GREG WAS STILL GRINNING when Laine disappeared into the bathroom, and he liked the feeling. As he got back into the rest of his clothes, he realized he did a lot of laughing and grinning around Laine. She made happiness bubble to the surface in him, made him want to do the same for her. The silliness they often exchanged was very precious to a man like him. Women usually wanted him to be charming instead, and never even considered silliness.

But the charm was false and the silliness real, and so was what he felt for Laine Randall. Sour skepticism tried to touch him again, but he firmly shook it off. If things didn't work out with Laine after all this was over, it wouldn't be because *he* didn't try.

"And where were *you* all night?" he heard suddenly, the demand wrenching him out of sweet thoughts about the future. Anita had just come through the door, and he hadn't even heard it opening. "Do you have any idea how long I waited? If you think I'm going to make appointments just to get to see you—"

"Keep it down, I have company," he cautioned low, by then close enough to redirect her entrance. "Believe it or not I've been working, and here's the latest."

He brought her up to date in the fewest possible words, including the discovery in the autopsy reports. She'd started out angry with him because she'd been worried, but strangely enough hearing about his attacker calmed her. If she'd been able to stay in the room across the hall...well, things had worked out well in spite of the difficulties.

"So I want you to pass on my report to Control," he finished up. "Tell them it might help to have our own team of pathologists on this, but at the very least we need a set of fingerprints from my late visitor. Doughnuts to jelly beans he's a pro who usually works for the Morescu."

"No bet," she answered with a soft laugh. "And I take it you'd prefer if I knocked the next time I came by?"

"Only if you want to continue among the living," he returned with a grin. "The choice is completely yours."

"Thanks, pal," she chuckled, then left the room more quietly than she'd arrived. She was still Greg's ace in the hole, and would stay as far undercover as possible until the assignment was over.

He was almost to the point of wondering what was taking Laine so long when she reappeared. Her smile made him want to give her a quick kiss as he headed for his own turn in the bathroom, but she veered off toward the phone before they could come together. He sighed at the near miss, decided to do better next time, then forgot about it.

When he came out, she was off the phone and deep in thought. He stopped to wave a hand in front of her unseeing eyes, and she blinked then smiled at him.

"Sorry about that," she apologized. "I was just wondering if I was being too hard on a fellow woman. Donald Meerson and his friend Sassy were sunning on the patio when I called. When Don asked her if she would talk to me, she began having hysterics and ran into the suite. He said she's been a basket case since the new bodies were found last night, and blessed the fact that this time it was someone else who found them."

"It looks like you won't be talking to her, then," Greg said, trying to share Laine's disappointment. "I know you wanted to, but you're not likely to be missing anything important. How much can you expect to get out of an hysteric?"

"Maybe an understanding of why some people act like that," she answered, annoyance in her eyes. "Everyone feels afraid at *some* time, but certain men and women seem to be professionals at it. They scream and bounce and run and yell, and on occasion even faint. I've always had the crazy idea they do it on purpose, just to get out of having to cope. It's so much easier making other people cope *for* you."

"Maybe the truth is they can't cope," Greg suggested, for some reason playing devil's advocate. "Not everyone can, you know, especially if they're deeply and personally involved. Not trying could be their way of saving their sanity."

"There's a big difference between trying and not making it," Laine disagreed firmly. "There's nothing that says you have to be strong enough to handle something, but how do you know you can't unless you try? Those who go in for hysterics don't want to try. They'd rather take the easy way out and con other people into doing it for them."

"Maybe you're right," Greg conceded to end the disagreement, then he smiled at her. "Right now I'm most interested in conning you into joining me for lunch. I'm so hungry, I'll probably have hysterics if you refuse."

"I'm hungry, too," she said with a distracted nod, doing nothing to pick up on the opening he'd given her. "Let's go now and get it over with. I want to spend some time this afternoon thinking."

"I hope one of the things you'll be thinking about will be dinner," he said, following as she headed for the door. "You'll be having it with me, of course, and I'll be sure to have new theories for you to pick apart. Afterward, we'll—"

"No, I'm having dinner with Don Meerson," she interrupted, sounding as though she hadn't heard most of what he'd said. "He promised to work on getting Sassy calmed down enough to join the party, so I agreed. He also wants to talk about the movie I'm thinking of doing."

"What movie is that?" Greg asked, wondering why he didn't put an arm around her as they walked toward the elevator. She was being perfectly open and straightforward, but he had the strangest feeling he was with Anita instead of Laine. A friend and co-worker, nothing more personally involved.

"It's the reason I'm here," she said, only glancing at him. "I've been offered the lead in a movie that will, for the most part, be shot at this resort. I came to look around before giving my final acceptance, and they want me badly enough to have agreed to wait. I'm telling you that because I noticed it wasn't in the file you have on me."

"Did seeing that file bother you?" Greg asked at once, wondering if *that* could be what was wrong. "I had to be sure of why you were in the middle of this, and I couldn't blackmail it out of you the way you did with me."

"Don't worry, Greg, we all do what we have to," she answered, giving him the saddest smile he'd ever seen. "I'd never hold it against you, not when I was the one who really started it. Let's go get that lunch."

By then they'd reached the lobby, and suddenly the sadness was gone. It was as if someone had waved a magic wand, and Laine was back to being cheerful and friendly and sharing.

But the magic wand had also waved away the very special Laine Greg had been starting to know. He spent their lunch together trying to fight off the cold illness growing in his middle, telling himself he was imagining things. When lunch was over and they'd gone their separate ways, he wasn't in the least convinced.

LAINE WENT BACK to her suite alone, ordered a pitcher of lemonade, then took it out to the patio to drink. She'd been trying to decide whether she was thinking or brooding, and having a cold drink in the heat of the day should have helped. Of course it didn't, and that provided a very strong hint.

But what else could she do but brood? The lemonade was nicely sweetened, but everything else she'd had to swallow had been sour. Once the mystery was solved Greg Williams would be gone out of her life—and she thought she had it solved.

Or at least part of it. She stretched out a little more on the lounge, trying to resolve her conflicting emotions. The idea of catching up with Nissa's murderers did more than delight her; she felt deep, grim satisfaction that they would not be getting away with it no matter *how* clever they'd been. She would snatch away whatever they were hoping to get, just as they'd snatched away a beautiful, harmless life.

But the accomplishment would be costly. Once she had the guilty trapped, Greg would be able to get the details on the rest of it. He would probably also be able to keep her part in the matter quiet, which would satisfy Bob's first, most urgent worry. Her producers would never know she'd been involved in another crime investigation. All debts would be paid, all questions answered—and then it would be time to go home. All alone.

"And this time you'll notice, won't you?" she whispered to herself, staring down into the green-blue water sparkling with sunshine in the pool. "You can have any man you like, all you have to do is crook a finger. The only one you can't have is the man you love. So much for the fairy-tale lives of stars."

Laine thought about crying, but reached for the phone instead. She needed her friend, Lieutenant Halloran at Hollywood PD, to do some digging for her. Once she explained why, she knew he wouldn't hesitate. Tonight would be the last night that could be called a full moon, and Laine was certain it wasn't meant to be wasted. She wouldn't be wasting it, either.

And once it was over she would have plenty of time to cry.

GREG WENT BACK to his room, spent some time going through employee files, and then found himself pacing. The business part of his mind had absorbed everything it should have, but the personal side of him...

Why had everything changed so abruptly between Laine and himself? One minute she was soft and loving in his arms, and the next there was an invisible wall around her. Friendly, cooperative, but don't touch. What had he done? What *hadn't* he done? How was he expected to figure that out and work on the case at the same time?

His pacing was interrupted by a knock at the door. Anita stood there with towels over her arm, and as she looked at him her brows rose.

"I can't be that much of a disappointment to you," she remarked. "I'm told I'm fairly good at my job. And I'm not Greek so you don't have to worry about the gift I'm bearing."

"What gift?" Greg asked with a frown as he stepped back to let her in. Maybe whatever it was would be able to distract him.

"They finally sent that major crimes list you wanted," she answered, pulling a thin pile of printout from between the towels she held. "They delayed sending it until they had it updated and complete, including the very latest. Yesterday morning an entire train was hijacked outside of Bucharest. No one's admitting there was anything special on the train, but there are more investigators in the area than anxious passenger relatives."

"That, happily, doesn't feel like it fits," Greg said, beginning to look through the printout. "Bank robbery, England. Bank robbery, France. Kidnapping, Belgium. Bank robbery, Italy. Stolen airliner, Saudi Arabia. Stolen radioactive waste, France. Bank robbery, Dakar. Stolen gold shipment, Switzerland—*that* must be embarrassing. The Swiss have a reputation to maintain."

"Do you have any idea what you're looking for?" Anita asked. "Amsterdam lost a large shipment of diamonds, Uganda a presold load of ivory, and there are rumors coming out of China about the disappearance of a priceless jade necklace. The only place not reporting major crimes these days is Transylvania. Do you think there's a connection *there?*"

"You have to try to remember we're involved with werewolves, not vampires," Greg answered absently. "If you keep confusing the two, you'll find yourself waving garlic when it ought to be silver. Some of these crimes are individual or small-party efforts. The rest have to be chalked up to large organizations, but the big groups seem to have stopped leaving notes. Isn't anyone into justifying their doings as world-saving any longer?"

"I think the airliner was taken by note-leavers," Anita replied with a frown as she searched her memory. "If I'm not mistaken, even the airline people laughed when they read it. They're not about to pay the equivalent of twenty million dollars for an old, empty plane. Whichever amateurs took it can keep it."

"And we're dealing with professionals rather than amateurs," Greg said with a sigh, closing the printout. "They have to be bringing *something* into this country, but we don't know what. It's worth a lot of money to whoever's buying, and also worth the risk of dealing with the Morescu. What could possibly be worth that much, and why are there werewolves mixed in?"

"Those are really good questions," Anita allowed soberly. "As soon as I have the answers, I'll be sure to let you know. Control has confirmed that the man who attacked you was a pro, and that he often contracted for the Morescu. They said he's been known to work with a partner, so they suggest you stay very alert. They don't want you caught in the middle and burned.''

"Right," Greg said sourly. "Caught in the middle and—"

And that was when he got it, all the clues, big and little, falling into place. He knew what they were bringing in, and why the Morescu had to be involved. The only thing he didn't know was who, but that bit of data would come soon enough.

"And they're taking your advice and sending in a team of our own pathologists," Anita went on, missing the look of revelation in his eyes. "The state authorities were wondering why the locals hadn't requested assistance with this mess, and were happy to intervene on our behalf. They'll stay well clear of *this* place to keep from stepping on our toes, but—"

"No, we don't want them doing that," Greg interrupted, suddenly brisk. "We'll need a special cordon around this place, and it'll take some arranging. I'll make the call and tell them what to look for, and then you and I have some research to do. With any luck, we'll have this cleared up by tomorrow."

"Hey, wait a minute," Anita protested, stopping him on the way to the phone. "I know you're the resident genius here, but how about giving me a hint about what's going on? Even the mad scientist shares secrets with Igor."

"And fair's fair," he agreed, pausing to smile at her. "You've been working on this, so you have a right to know. Okay, here's how I see it. The Morescu had to be involved because of what was being smuggled in—radioactive waste. What the printout said was stolen from France.''

"Hold it," Anita said, shaking her head. "Not only don't I see how you got that, I can't even see a reason. Don't we have enough radioactive waste here in this country?''

"That's the whole trouble," Greg said with a nod. "We have so much of it here, every gram can be accounted for. If some of it was missing, everyone would know it was stolen even if they didn't know who got it. Whoever started this wants to use the stuff in some way, but obviously doesn't want others to know they're doing it. That's why it was stolen in Europe and is being smuggled in.''

"And they needed the Morescu both to do the stealing and to do the smuggling," Anita said with a thoughtful nod of her own. "Okay, I've picked up that part of the trail. Now tell me how you know it's being smuggled in.''

"Laine and I read the autopsy reports," Greg said, sitting down on the arm of a couch. "The old ME noted that there were masked surgical scars, which meant nothing until I realized that the incisions could have been made when something was put *into* those people, not taken out. And one of them had slight tissue burns, which could have been caused by radioactive leakage from a damaged lead container. The container would have to be very small to fit into a relatively small incision, so it was probably damaged while it was being inserted.''

"I don't believe anyone would let that be done to them," Anita said, her voice fainter to match the way she'd paled a little. "Smuggle radioactive waste into this country in their own bodies? And take the chance of a leak, which *did* happen in one case? And what about airport security? The lead containers would set off every alarm they went past.''

"Lead won't set off airport security,'' Greg assured her. "Not even if there were ten times as much. The detectors aren't set up for it. And the reason those people allowed it was because they were all dying. If a man or woman has nothing to leave their family after they're gone, dying isn't the worst thing they face. They'd willingly give up the rest of their time if it meant their family could be left financially secure. The Morescu supplied the money, they supplied the bodies.''

"Yes, desperation makes people do things they'd never consider doing under other circumstances,'' Anita agreed with reluctance. "It's just so...*cold-blooded,* committing suicide in that particular way. And that's what it was, suicide. They had to know they would be killed—but wait a minute. Why couldn't the lead containers simply be taken out of them the same way they were put in? That way no one would have known.''

"I would guess they didn't want to take any chances,'' Greg said, rubbing at his face. "They were dealing with dying people, remember. If even two of their couriers died too soon, the autopsy reports would be looked at by too many people. Officials in this country are very careful about foreign nationals who die here; they have to know what killed the person and if it's contagious. Embassies from the countries of origin have to know what killed one of their own, just to be certain there's no convenient cover-up if someone important should later ask. A thorough autopsy would reveal too many unanswered questions, so they've just been playing it safe."

"The people who started this have to be at least as bad as the Morescu, if not worse," Anita stated, holding down a shudder. "Now you can go ahead and make your call. The sooner they're caught, the happier I'll be."

Greg put a hand to her arm in silent understanding, then continued on his way to the phone. His earlier briskness had turned to eagerness, but not of the usual sort. This time he wanted the assignment over and out of the way for personal reasons, which he intended to get to the minute business was taken care of.

If he let Laine Randall go without a fight, he deserved to lose her.

Chapter Nineteen

The afternoon passed fairly quickly for Laine. She took refuge from the world in a nap until Lieutenant Halloran called back with the information she needed, and then she went to dress for dinner. She was expected at Don's dinner party about seven, but being a few minutes late wouldn't be a problem. Not unexpectedly she'd dreamed about Greg, and she wanted a bath to soak away the memory.

The dress for that night was already picked out, so once her makeup and hair were done she got into it. It happened to be a Salla Loren original in rose silk, the very full skirt deliberately above the knee and belted with wide silver chain links. The bodice had a deep, silver-laced V-neck, and the long sleeves were very wide and closed at the cuffs with silver buttons. A filigreed silver pendant and matching earrings went on next, and then the silver-heeled rose sling-backs. The silver purse was a delicately chained shoulder bag, and that made the ensemble complete.

"This outfit should freak out every werewolf in a fifty-mile radius," she muttered to her reflection in the mirror. "Every bit of this silver is real, except for the purse. I wonder if anyone will get the message."

It was impossible to know, but shouldn't take too long to find out. In a matter of hours... Well, no use just standing there. Right then she was no more than fashionably late; even if she'd wanted to drag her feet, the time to do it was past.

Donald Meerson's suite wasn't all that far from Laine's, and she spent the walk over relaxing into the part she would play. Polite, friendly, eager to discuss everything about werewolves, open, faintly silly...just about the way she'd been last night. No one seemed to think she was behaving out of character except Bob, but he knew her a good deal better. With him safely out of the way, there shouldn't be a problem.

Her ring at the door brought an immediate answer, but not by her host. Some of the hotel people had been hired to serve at the dinner, and one of them was obviously also taking care of arriving guests. More than a half dozen people stood in the living room not far from the large dining table that had been set up, and one of them was Don Meerson. As soon as he saw Laine he greeted her, then began introducing her to the others.

It didn't take long before everyone was seated, and dinner was a sumptuous affair. Don apologized for Sassy's absence, telling everyone she was resting and trying to pull herself together. They were scheduled to leave the following day, and neither of them regretted that.

After dinner everyone was offered liqueurs and brandy out on the patio, and soft music played in the background. Two of the staff people stayed to serve them while the others cleared away the remnants of the meal. By the time the table and chairs and leftovers were gone, so were the other guests. They'd spent most of the evening talking about the casino, and were finally unable to resist its lure.

"Fools in a hurry to throw away their money," Don Meerson said with a superior smile after the door was closed behind the last of them. "I don't mind trying my hand every once in a while, but I save the real money for important things. Would you like another liqueur, my dear?"

"I'm fine, thank you," Laine said with a shake of her head. "And by important things, I assume you mean investing in movies. What do you do to earn the real money, Don?"

"I'm in the contracting business," he answered with another smile, sitting down in the chair opposite hers. "Right now I'm negotiating for some important government contracts for two of my businesses, and when I get those I'll really be sitting pretty. I'll have enough to invest in a half dozen movies."

"Like the one I'm thinking about doing now?" she asked, putting aside her glass. The two staff people, not having been dismissed, stood separately at a discreet distance from their conversation. "You mentioned it when I called this afternoon, Don. Were you the one who insisted I star in it?"

"No, I put my money in when I heard the other backers were insisting on it," he answered with a grin that made him look somewhat boyish. "That way I got what I wanted without having to insist. The bunch of them were smart enough to know the script was all but written for you. No one else would be as perfect."

"And that, of course, explains most of what was confusing me," Laine said, her nod satisfied. "I wondered how you knew about the movie, since most people don't. You know because you have money invested in it, and because you're the one who suggested this location."

"What makes you think I suggested this location?" he asked. The words were easy, but he no longer looked at all boyish. "I'm not the only investor who's been here before, you know, or even the only one involved with the movie. Once we read the script, it was more of a group decision."

"No, *you* were the one who first suggested it," Laine disagreed. "Everyone else went along, but the idea was yours. Enough people remember that, so there's no confusion."

"Even if that's true, what difference would it make?" he asked, crossing his legs as he leaned back. "I don't remember making the suggestion, but so what if I did?"

"It was the first of your mistakes," she answered, feeling the way he was now drawing back on the inside. "You had already arranged to use this place for another reason, and you never should have mixed the two. Just the way you should never have given in to the urge to get to know me better. And boast about insider knowledge. That part of it was really stupid."

"I still don't know what you're talking about," he growled, beginning to flush. "And if you think you can sit there and insult me—"

"Insult you?" Laine barked out a laugh. "How do you insult the sort of garbage *you* are? The only way you could get what you wanted was to have people die, and it didn't bother you in the least to add an innocent name to the list. But Nissa wasn't really all that innocent, was she? Your–'associates' killed her because she was a danger to you, not because she just happened to be in the wrong place at the wrong time. I wasn't certain about that until this evening, but now I'm positive.''

"Something's got you so upset, you're making wild accusations," Meerson said soothingly, beginning to reach into his white dinner jacket. "Let me—"

"Go right ahead," Laine invited, the automatic from her purse now solidly in her hand. "Give me the excuse I've been praying for. You have no idea how much I want it."

And that was an understatement. If Laine hadn't had rigid control over herself, she would have been trembling violently with rage. This was the man who was responsible for Nissa's death, and she wanted his own life so badly it frightened her to the soul. Her fingers ached to squeeze the trigger, and something deep inside said she'd never regret it.

"Everyone said Nissa was killed only because she happened to be there," Laine related in a desperate effort to distract herself. "It was so reasonable an explanation even *I* believed it—until other things happened that didn't make sense. That business with the werewolf, and the fact that I was investigating it."

She stared at Meerson's pallid face as she fought to put it all into words.

"Someone had gone to a lot of trouble to suggest that a werewolf was responsible for the murders," Laine continued to her silent, captive audience. "When I began investigating the werewolf question, those responsible should have been pleased. It was suggested that they *were* pleased, and were only pretending that they wanted me to stop. After all, those attackers were under orders not to hurt me badly. My friend and bodyguard was only drugged rather than killed, and a rabbit was torn apart instead of me.

"But that didn't make any sense. If clues suggesting a werewolf were left deliberately, what could stopping my investigation hope to hide? And if I was being encouraged rather than discouraged, why two episodes? Why press the point and take the chance of actually scaring me off?

"That was when I decided someone *didn't* want me investigating, and there was a very good reason for wanting to stop me. No official agency would ever admit they had werewolf murders on their hands, even if they were personally convinced that that was the explanation. They would putter around and file empty reports, then let the matter drop as soon as they possibly could. If word got out they would look like morons, and that would be the end of their careers.

"But then *I* came along, and didn't worry about looking ridiculous. I went around questioning people, which could have brought to light a witness capable of refuting the theory. At that point the police would have been back in with reinforcements, and that was what the murderers had been trying to avoid. I had to be stopped, and as quickly as possible."

Laine noticed the surrounding silence then, no more than night sounds as the backdrop to her narrative. Meerson stared at her expressionlessly, but the touch of fear lurked in his eyes.

"So the attempts to stop me were real, but now they really didn't make any sense," Laine continued. "By the time of the second attempt, four people had already been killed. Just this morning a fifth was attempted, but not once was I in any serious danger. Someone suggested the guilty party was a fan of mine, but why should that include Bob Samson? Why hadn't *he* been killed, as thoughtlessly as Nissa had been tossed out of the way?

"I was very confused, and the feeling extended even to my investigation. There was exactly one person at this resort who claimed to have seen something relating to werewolves, but she refused to talk to me. She'd mentioned her story to anyone willing to listen, including the police; when it came to repeating it to me, though, she was unavailable. Her nerves were shot, I was told, and she was too frightened to go into details."

"So what's that supposed to prove?" Meerson asked, finally breaking his silence. "How hard is it to freak out a fluffhead? You don't think I have her with me because of her high IQ, do you? As soon as we get back to L.A. I'll be dumping her."

"Nice try, but it won't work," Laine said, the faint smile she now wore feeling out of place. "You want to put the blame on Sassy and walk away clean, but that simply isn't possible. Your girlfriend 'saw' something to help along the werewolf story, but she didn't do it for herself. *You* couldn't have claimed to have seen something without making the police suspicious, and your denying the story added to it. Only one person who saw something, one person no one believed—the scenario is classic."

"And yours is pure imagination," he countered with a snort, beginning to lean forward. "It's only—"

"It's the final puzzle piece," Laine interrupted, bringing up the gun again. "Along with the fact that you're involved in the movie. I wasn't killed because I'm the one who will make that movie into a moneymaker instead of a tax loss; Bob wasn't killed because he's the only assistant director Farring is currently willing to work with. Without a competent assistant director Farring will ruin the movie, but he's already under contract. You need us both, or your investment is down the drain.''

Meerson froze at the movement of the gun, and once again he was silent. The fear had intensified in his eyes, and that gave Laine grim satisfaction.

''You were at a party with us somewhere, so you know Bob drinks Scotch while I don't,'' she went on. ''And the final point is that Nissa was killed because she recognized your scatterbrained girlfriend. You needed someone who could be counted on to play the part of a trembling witness properly, so you brought along an actress. Sassy is a professional who Nissa recognized immediately, so Nissa had to go. You were afraid *I* would recognize her also, and that's why she disappeared every time I came around. The only thing she's afraid of is getting caught in her act—even though she already made one bad slip.''

Her listener frowned, the involuntary action telling Laine he was getting nervous.

''She claimed she saw a shadow, a grotesque shape that wasn't a man,'' Laine clarified. ''That part of the story must have been prepared before it started raining, to point up the full moon part of the background. It sounds scary as hell, but would you like to tell me what produced that shadow? The only light source near enough was the light over the call box. Clouds covered any moonlight there might have been, and pouring rain tends to destroy shadows.''

Meerson had grown pale, since it wasn't possible to doubt Laine's reconstruction. The muscles in his jaws jumped as he ground his teeth, and desperation crept into his stare. If she hadn't been holding a gun on him, Laine knew he would have been long since out of his chair.

"The only thing I don't know is exactly how Nissa caught you," she added. "Did she walk onto the scene while you and Sassy were watching that man being killed by one of your Morescu associates, or did she simply see Sassy getting ready to be professionally hysterical? I have this theory about hysterics—but I know you two didn't commit the murders with your own hands, because you had no blood on you. You may remember that I was right there when you and Sassy burst in with your news. I couldn't see her face behind her hands, and then *I* left to visit the murder scene."

Memory of that soul-wrenching time came back to Laine, and Donald Meerson must have seen it in her eyes. Growing terror sent his flickering glance to the weapon in her hand, and suddenly he was on his feet.

"So you've come here to kill me," he challenged, trying to sound brave even though he was rooted to the spot. Laine had risen no more than an instant after him, and the gun she held still didn't waver. "You're looking for an excuse, you said, but you really don't intend waiting for one. You're going to kill me no matter what I do."

"I'd like to," Laine answered, telling the absolute truth. "I want to kill you as casually as you had Nissa killed, and I'm not worried about it bothering my conscience. The difference between you and me, though, is that I've learned to live in our society, not simply use it. Now that I've caught you, I'll let society settle your hash."

"And that's *your* major mistake," Meerson said, no longer looking frightened. He'd turned positively gleeful, and Laine couldn't understand that until she felt something hard jabbed into her back. "You should have pulled that trigger first thing, while you still could," he gloated. "Now you'll drop the gun."

"You've seen too many bad movies," Laine answered at once, ignoring her pounding heart and dry mouth. Those waiters . . . it had to be one of them behind her. "If he shoots me, I'll do the same favor for you before the lights go out. Since you're the boss, tell him to drop his gun and come around to where I can see him."

"Oh, what a pity to waste such excellent lines," another male voice chimed in from the door to the suite on Laine's left. Meerson had paled again, but hadn't had the chance to say anything. "The only problem with that is, Don *isn't* the boss. *I* am, and if necessary I'm prepared to lose him."

Laine knew that voice, and also knew the man wasn't joking. He'd obviously been playing a part the last time she'd spoken to him, but not now. The easy authority in his tone said he was telling the complete truth, and then the question was settled for her. A hand reached around from behind her to the right, and the automatic was yanked out of her loosened grip.

And that, of course, meant she was in deep, deep trouble.

GREG SPENT THE REST of the day getting things organized. He was so busy he barely had time to grab something for dinner, and that was a blessing. He was also too busy to think about Laine. Or almost too busy. If nothing else he wanted her in on the last of that case, but she had gone to a dinner party.

When he finally had the time, he called her suite. It was still fairly early, so he wasn't surprised when he got no answer. But as more time passed and he still hadn't been able to reach her, he began to feel uneasy. At the very least, she would have let him know whether or not she'd spoken to Sassy.

"Unless she took her werewolf research in another direction," he muttered, running a hand through his hair. "Why do I have the feeling I shouldn't have let her out of my sight?"

Because she can't be trusted not to put her beautiful neck on the chopping block, his mind immediately replied.

"I've got to find her," he decided aloud, no longer worried about talking to himself. At that point he had every right to talk to himself. A lesser man would be banging his head against a wall, but not Greg Williams. He just talked to himself while checking the clip in his gun, then quickly left the room.

People in evening clothes milled around the lobby, some standing talking, others drifting in or out. The major topic of conversation was whether or not there would be any more murders, and Greg knew the attitude would have upset Laine. Those people were hanging around *hoping* there would be new bodies. Greg pitied them. Why kill yourself to amass incredible amounts of money, when the one thing a fortune most often brought with it was boredom?

Greg pushed through the doors into the cooling darkness, thinking how lucky he was to have a job he loved. It made him want to get up in the morning, eager to find out what the new day would hold. It hadn't done much for his love life, but what he did was part of who he was. When a woman rejected his work, she was also rejecting the basic man.

Which, Greg admitted to himself as he looked around, wasn't all that hard to understand. Granted, his job didn't always land him in the middle of violence, but there was enough of it to bother any normal woman.

At that point he was close to Laine's suite, the first place he'd planned to search for her. But he suddenly found himself stopped, in a violent way. This time the person coming up behind him made no sound at all; the first hint Greg had was when the garrote settled around his throat.

Greg immediately tried to reach his attacker or his holstered weapon, but the person behind him was a pro. The knee in his back gave the strangler more leverage on the cord, while at the same time keeping his attacker out of easy reach. This time Greg was meant to die.

Blackness began to close in on him, a darkness that usually brought weakness and eventual unconsciousness. Greg knew that he mustn't give in to it or he was done for, but he couldn't breathe ... or fight ... or stand ...

Chapter Twenty

And then the deadly pressure was gone, released as suddenly as it had come. Greg was down on his knees, and as soon as he pulled the cord free he began gulping in air. He still felt the urge to pass out, but refused to give in to it. He needed to be conscious now, and that's what he *would* be.

"Are you all right?" a deep voice asked, and then a hand came to his arm. "Don't try to stand up yourself. Let me help you."

Greg needed that help, but once he was erect the strength began coming back to him. He looked around to see an unconscious man on the ground, one who was dressed all in dark colors. He remembered then that his first attacker often worked with a partner, and silently cursed himself for having forgotten. If not for a surprising, unexpected intervention, the slip could have killed him.

"It's fairly obvious I owe you more than simple thanks," Greg said, finally looking at his rescuer. "I also owe you my apologies for having thought you were involved in all this. I'm glad you're the forgiving sort, Mr. Samson."

"Call me Bob," the man answered, taking the hand that was being offered to him. "And there was nothing to be forgiving about. I didn't know I was one of your suspects, Mr. Williams, so no harm done. Or at least not to anyone who didn't deserve it."

His glance touched the unconscious man briefly, making Greg smile.

"I couldn't agree more, Bob, and I'd appreciate you calling me Greg. But how did you happen to turn up so conveniently? My luck doesn't usually run quite this good."

"Luck has nothing to do with it," Bob answered, looking worried. "I was on my way to find you, when I saw you leave the main building. When you reached the suite I would have taken you quietly aside, but then *that* guy came out of the shadows. I had no idea he was there, or I would have shouted a warning."

"What's wrong?" Greg demanded, knowing immediately that the problem had to do with Laine. "What's happened to her?"

"I'm hoping I'm worried about nothing," Bob said, but he obviously didn't believe he was. "I followed her to Meerson's suite and watched people show up for his dinner party, but I also watched everyone leave again. The only one who didn't leave was Laine, but maybe she's just visiting. She doesn't *have* to be in trouble, does she?"

"Of course not," Greg said with a definite sinking feeling inside him. "And the check really could be in the mail, but it isn't very likely. We'd better get over there and find out."

He turned away from Bob to retrieve the cord he had almost been strangled with, and used it to tie his attacker's hands behind his back. He also relieved the unconscious man of the knife he carried, wishing he had the time to call Anita. If the man awoke before anyone official found him, he would be gone despite being tied.

"Okay, let's go," he said to Bob as he straightened. If the choice was between keeping a man in custody and saving Laine's life, it could go only one way for Greg. If the man was lost, it would be possible to find him again; if Laine's life was lost...

The two of them hurried through the darkness to the suite that Bob said was Meerson's, and then Greg led the way around to the back. They had to see what was going on before anyone saw *them,* and Bob was a good fellow skulker. He made no more noise than Greg did, which let them push through the corner of the hedge where the branches were thin. No one heard or saw them, but there was certainly something for *them* to see.

Even as they watched, a uniformed man with a gun in Laine's back took her own weapon from her hand. She'd been holding it on Meerson, who sagged down into the chair behind him. Another uniformed man stood to the left, behind the one who had Laine covered. Over near the door to the suite stood three people who couldn't easily be seen, a female and two males. This wasn't good, and it wasn't likely to get any better.

"Stay here in the shadows," Greg whispered almost soundlessly to Bob. "I'm going to get in closer the fastest way possible, but that will put me at a disadvantage. If I haven't figured out something to do and started doing it in five minutes, get out of here and call the sheriff. If the fun starts before then, feel free to join in."

Bob nodded silently, his lack of argument a pleasant contrast to the way Laine would have done it. But Greg still wished it was Laine beside him, instead of over there with those...

He took his 9MM firmly in his fist, then stepped out of the darkness to the edge of the pool.

"HOLD IT RIGHT THERE," Laine heard from her right, and joined everyone else in looking in that direction. It really was Greg, she saw to her vast relief, not just wishful thinking on her part. He'd come to her rescue again.

"No, *you* hold it," Donald Meerson shouted back, charging to his feet in what almost looked like a rage. "We have a gun in Laine Randall's back, and that means you have five seconds to get rid of yours. If you don't, she's dead. One...two...three..."

"All right!" Greg yelled, tossing his gun away like an idiot. "I got rid of it. Just don't hurt her."

"She'll be fine—for now," Meerson responded with surprised pleasure. "Come over here and join us, Mr. Williams."

Laine groaned to herself as Greg circled the pool and came closer, for that minute wishing she'd been smart enough to get involved with Dirty Harry instead of Gentleman Greg. Harry would have known that throwing his gun away was suicide, and that no matter *what* threat...

"Well, well, it looks like we're all here," Greg said, glancing around at the people who stared at him. "I would guess you're Donald Meerson, those two are plug-uglies on loan from the Morescu, and the girl is the much-mentioned Sassy. I don't know the names of your other two friends, though."

"Ralph van Ort and Jeremy Roberts," the first man supplied as he stepped forward with a very pretty redhead and the man Greg had faced down the night before. "But don't bother trying to remember the names. In a very short while you won't be remembering anything at all."

His smile lent a certain aristocratic shadow to his otherwise pleasant expression, an enjoyment of the fact that he no longer needed to remain in the background. Jeremy's grin made his handsomeness dazzling, and the redhead beside him showed the superior smile of one who hadn't the least amount of conscience. Laine wanted to jump up and down on all their faces, but they were certain to have plans precluding that.

"I can see you weren't just gossiping last night, Ralph," Laine commented as evenly as possible. "All that help you gave me about Sassy and what she'd seen—you did it on purpose."

"Of course," the man answered with a warm smile, once again looking like your average guy. "I had Jeremy ready to take you out of the way for a while, but just in case it didn't work I wanted another chance at you. What better place than right here, the suite of my junior associate? I knew we'd find out if you were really dangerous to us if we got you here, and we did."

"Speaking of plans not working, you're not whining any more, Roberts," Greg commented, his tone downright condescending. "Is that because no one is hurting your poor little arm any longer?"

"I thought I did that rather well," Jeremy said with a laugh, surprising Laine by not being angry. "At my belt level I could have taken you apart, Williams, but that wasn't the place to make a scene. Before this is over, we'll have to find a place."

"What's wrong with right here and now?" Greg asked, only his light eyes showing that he'd expected Jeremy to lose his temper. "Your game is all finished, you know, so if you don't take advantage of *this* chance, you probably won't get another."

"But our game isn't anywhere near finished," Jeremy disagreed with another laugh. "Ralph, Donald and I have gotten only three of the six shipments, so the werewolf will have to claim his last three victims tonight. After that we'll be gone, and the werewolf will go with us. You two will just disappear."

"How do you expect to get the radioactives past the cordon I've had set up around the area?" Greg asked very mildly, just as though he were discussing the weather. "My people have very sensitive detectors, so the smallest leak through the lead coverings will be enough to locate the material no matter where you put it. And that goes for whether or not you get to the last three couriers."

By then Jeremy Roberts was no longer laughing, Donald Meerson was back to looking pale and Ralph van Ort was furious. They glanced at one another with a grimness that was downright frightening, and then Ralph jerked forward toward Greg.

"How did you know?" he demanded harshly, his eyes bright with rage. "No one could have figured out our plan, no one! Who the hell are you?"

"No one," Greg answered with an insolent grin. "Or, to be more exact, the no one who also arranged to have your bought coroner taken into custody. You know, the man who removed the lead containers from the dead bodies as he autopsied them? He was also supposed to make sure nothing suspicious showed up in his reports, while at the same time silently blaming a werewolf. A shame he was too slow to handle the rush, and the old coroner was brought out of retirement to help him. Were you the one responsible for the unexpected inheritance that let the old coroner retire just at *this* time? Silly question, of course you were."

Greg beamed at van Ort and Roberts, obviously trying to goad one of the furious men into attacking him. Laine hoped with everything in her that he would succeed, but the obnoxious pair refused to cooperate. Van Ort put a restraining hand on Roberts's arm, then took a deep breath.

"There's still a way out of this," he said, just as though he were thinking aloud. "The woman came here to confront the murderer of her friend, but she didn't tell you about it first. If she had, you would have come with lots of backup, not all alone. Your people may know what, but they don't know who. If we dispose of you two and play it cool, we'll just be four more faces out of the hundreds here. I like that, so we'll go with it."

His smile was benevolent and friendly, with nothing in it to show he'd just pronounced a death sentence on them. Laine glanced at Greg, hoping he was planning to do something, but the sickened frustration in his expression said he was out of ideas. Laine would have been frantic if she'd had the time; instead, she launched into the lunatic idea *she'd* gotten, doing it quickly before she realized how little chance it had.

"You missed a very important point," she said to Ralph van Ort, taking one carefully planned step forward. "I didn't just come here to avenge the death of my friend. My second reason makes all the difference."

"The difference in what?" the man asked with a snort, his eyes moving slowly over her. "If you expect to bargain for your life—"

"You really are stupid," she interrupted with an amused laugh, but one that was on the fey side. "You thought the only ones you had to worry about were the authorities, that you could use the idea of werewolves without anyone caring. I hate to tell you this, but someone does care."

"Someone?" Ralph echoed, his smile fading slightly. "Who could you possibly be referring—"

"Don't you know how much trouble you've made for us, you fool?" Laine said in a near growl. "Especially since this isn't the first time? How long did you expect us to let it go on?"

Van Ort lost his amusement entirely at the cold, strange way she was looking at him. She stood easily and gazed at him without fear, hardly the behavior of someone who was moments away from death...

"What—what are you talking about?" he asked after swallowing, the shadow of suspicion turning his mouth dry. "How did you know about the other time, and who do you mean by 'we'?"

"You know who I mean," she answered, her voice beginning to sound breathy, and almost echoing. "We've worked very hard to keep our presence quiet, to take for our needs only those who would never be missed. But you—you come along and ruin it all, make people think about us...think seriously without scoffing...put them on their guard..."

Her breathing was definitely on the heavy side now, and something seemed to be happening to her beautiful face. It was as though she were trying to keep it from stretching.

"We decided to thank you for that in the most appropriate way possible," she went on in a raspy whisper that somehow carried to all of them there. "This is one beyond the true night...the need to change less demanding...but still there...and so happily given in to..."

Van Ort watched in horror as she went to one knee on the concrete, her arms wrapped around herself, her hair thrown forward over her bent head to hide her face. The small hairs at the back of his neck stood at attention— And then the most ghastly howl sounded from the back of the patio near the hedge, an inhuman howl from one of her inhuman associates!

"My God, there's more of them," one of the two guards in serving uniform choked out, his voice absolutely terrified. The words seemed to wake the second guard out of deep shock, and with a whimpered scream he dropped the guns he held and ran. Van Ort had also lost to the fever of fear, and when the other two broke he found it impossible to stand his ground. The first guard was with the second by the time they reached the door to the suite, a trembling van Ort no more than a pace behind. The three quickly disappeared inside and slammed the door shut behind them.

Laine looked up in time to see Greg charging at Jeremy Roberts, which quickly broke the spell for the second man. With a snarled curse he grabbed a gibbering Donald Meerson and threw the smaller man at Greg, then dove for the guns the guard had dropped.

Laine had her sling-backs off in an instant, but she didn't have to try to stop Jeremy herself. Greg helped Meerson stumble past him with a push, and then *he* was after Jeremy. Greg reached him, and the two came together with a crash and rolled. Since she now stood straight again, Laine could see that neither of them had gotten a weapon.

Which was something that Sassy had also noticed. She circled the two struggling men with a look of fury on her face, a full partner in that horror about to shift the balance of power back to her own side. With the men fighting to her right and Laine's left, she had a clear run at her intentions.

Or so she thought. Laine was no more than an instant behind her in moving, and when Sassy reached the guns, Laine reached her. Just as she began straightening with a weapon in her hand, Laine's fist smashed into her face. She screeched and went over backward, and the gun went flying from her fingers.

Laine was busy trying to shake the pain out of her hand, but she felt so good she didn't mind the pain. She'd been too furious to hit the other woman properly, but it didn't matter in the least. That one had been for Nissa and Greg.

"That's more than enough," a wild voice growled, and Laine looked around to see something that made her heart sink. Jeremy Roberts had somehow gotten the gun Sassy had lost, and he stood there pointing it at Greg. Jeremy's face was cut and bruised, and Greg didn't have a scratch. So much for Jeremy's so-called high belt level then, but that made it worse. He now had another score to settle.

"You two have ruined things for us," he accused, dividing his dark stare between Laine and a standing Greg. "You've made us lose it all, so I'm going to return the favor. Our last gift to you will be a bullet,

Williams, but the next to last will be *her* body. Stand there and watch while I kill her.''

Jeremy began shifting the gun in an arc, pointing it at Laine, and this time she knew he would shoot. If she could have jumped out of the way she would have, but there was nowhere to jump *to*. Instead she refused to show how hard she was trembling inside, and simply stood there with her head high. The slime might kill her, but he would *not* have the satisfaction of seeing her collapse. But she had to look at Greg one last time...

And then it was over in a way Laine hadn't anticipated. Jeremy stood with most of his body facing Greg, a posture that would have let him bring the gun back fast if necessary. Greg didn't move from where he stood, but he did move. His hand went to the back of his waist, the arm blurred back and then forward, and a sickening thud came. Laine looked over to see the handle of a knife sticking out of Jeremy's chest, and Jeremy collapsing to the ground...

Things blurred just a little after that, and when the fog cleared Laine discovered she was sitting in a chair. Somehow Bob had gotten there, and he stood holding a gun on a thoroughly defeated Don and Sassy.

Greg came out of the suite and headed directly for Laine, but there was a strange expression on his face. She was still trying to adjust to the fact that they weren't dead, but she did notice that he stopped a foot away. Rather than come closer and take her in his arms...

"Are you all right?" he asked quietly, crouching down to look up at her. "You had a nasty shock, so don't worry about feeling shaky."

"Tell me about it," Laine muttered, never having felt anything like this before. She'd been so close to dying, she'd almost been able to see her newspaper obituary. "But how about *you?* Did he hurt you at all? And where did Bob come from?"

"He wasn't good enough to hurt me," Greg answered with a faint smile. "That's why he grabbed the gun when it all but fell into his hands. And Bob's the one who told me where you were, and that you were probably in trouble. He also supplied the werewolf howl just when we needed it."

"Yes, I remember now," Laine exclaimed, wondering how she could have forgotten. The timing of it had been so right it had even frightened *her.* "I had no idea where it came from, but it certainly did the trick."

"No, you did the trick," he disagreed. "I was absolutely certain you were just acting, but you went from human to inhuman so quickly and thoroughly—even knowing better, I found myself believing everything you said. When you crouched I *knew* you were about to change, and that howl nearly sent me over the edge. When I saw the two heavies panic and run, I was really tempted to join them."

"But you didn't," she said softly, wishing he was close enough for her to touch him. "You stayed instead, and then you—"

She'd been about to say, "closed the case," but that was so soulless. She wanted to say, "saved my life," but it probably would have embarrassed him. That meant she didn't know *what* to say, and then they were interrupted.

The sheriff and his deputies poured out of the suite, the presence of a few plainclothes people a circumstance they weren't noticing. They spread out to various places across the patio, and the sheriff himself came over to them with a big grin on his face.

"You were right, Williams," he began without preamble. "Tonight's killings were scheduled for an out of the way place we wouldn't be covering, and we found it and got them all. The 'werewolf' came equipped with steel claws and a spray desensitizer—he numbed his victims' throats with a spray anesthetic, so when he ripped their throats out it didn't hurt them. Nice of them to be so concerned."

"Most suicidal people don't want pain," Greg commented as he straightened to his feet. "Those couriers were all committing suicide by letting themselves be killed, most probably for the money to give to their families. Van Ort didn't want them backing out through fear of pain. But that reminds me, Laine. How did you know they'd done this sort of thing before? Your saying that helped van Ort to believe you."

"I was guessing," Laine answered with a shrug as she stood. "He was so outraged that you'd figured out what he was doing, it came to me that it had probably been tried before and had worked without a hitch. If something this complex goes bad the first time you try it, you curse the plan and bad luck. You only feel outrage if something workable has been ruined."

"Looks like I'll have to spread the word to other states," Sheriff Stoddard said, not at all reluctant. "Wherever that other jurisdiction is, they'll feel like fools for having gotten taken in. What I still don't understand is why they went to all this trouble. Wouldn't it have been easier to take these people away, kill them quietly, then hide the bodies? That way, who would have known?"

"The Immigration Department, for starters," Greg answered. "If foreign nationals began disappearing, you can bet they would investigate. And if even a single body turned up, that would be the end of the game. There's too much an autopsy can reveal, so you *want* an autopsy done, but by your own man. Along with an investigation that nobody wants to pursue, you have a neat little plan."

"This has to be why they didn't want Miss Randall poking around," Stoddard said with a thoughtful nod. "There's no way *we* would have investigated the possibility of a werewolf, but she was breaking the pattern."

"Roberts came after her last night in an effort to stop that," Greg supplied. "I thought he was simply making a nasty pass at her, but there was more involved. Bob Samson was watching her, so they locked him in the men's room. It probably annoyed the hell out of them when *I* showed up and ruined the scheme. That's why they tried to get me out of the way, so they could try again and this time succeed."

"But why would they smuggle in radioactive waste?" Stoddard demanded. "Don't we have enough of that gunk in *this* country? As a matter of fact, we probably have more of it than any other country you can name."

"But we're also very careful with it." Greg repeated what he'd told Anita for the sheriff's benefit. "If you wanted to steal some for a plan you had, you'd find it easier going in Europe. The Morescu, caring nothing about what it would be used for, would steal it and sell it to you. Other organizations would probably refuse to touch it."

"And I bet I know in general what they were going to use it for," Laine said as a sudden thought came to her. "Don Meerson told me he was expecting to win some very important government contracts. What better way to win a contract than to have your chief competition get caught being careless with radioactive waste? Who would believe that someone had framed them with smuggled-in waste?"

"Only somebody who also believed in were-wolves," Stoddard said with a wider grin. "I think from now on I'm going to have to stop worrying about looking like a fool. When you do that, you end up acting like one instead. We still have to catch up with Van Ort and the two heavies, but that shouldn't take long. And I'll need statements from the both of you, but that can wait until tomorrow."

He tipped his hat to them and went to join his men, leaving behind something of a silence. Laine looked around to find Greg staring at her, but as soon as their eyes met he glanced away.

"I still have details and paperwork to see to, so why don't you let Bob take you back to your suite," he said. The area they stood in seemed really fascinating, so much so that he couldn't stop looking at it.

"That sounds like a good idea," she agreed, fighting with all her strength to keep her voice even. He was trying to free himself from her with the least amount of trouble, and she owed him that much.

"See you around," he said in a lame way as she turned to find her shoes and purse. He sounded about as convincing as a novice reciting Shakespeare, but she went along with the lie and nodded. Once she left there, she knew she would never see Greg Williams again.

Bob was beside her by the time she had her possessions, and she let him take her arm to guide her through the army of officials. The way cleared once they were inside the suite, and Laine couldn't help glancing back one last time. Greg still stood where she'd left him, but he seemed to be lost in thought. So quickly, then, he'd forgotten all about her.

Without a sound, Laine continued on out.

Chapter Twenty-one

Greg Williams stood with head down and hands in pockets, unable to face the pain of watching Laine Randall walk out of his life. Part of him wanted to scream in torment and maybe even tear something apart, but he knew there had already been too much violence. The last of it had completely destroyed any chance he might have had with her, but what choice had he been given?

In his mind's eye, Greg saw again the shock on Laine's face when he'd killed Jeremy Roberts with the knife he'd taken from Roberts's second assassin. It was either that or let the man kill Laine, but many people see nothing but the act. Greg didn't blame her for being horrified, just as so many other women had been.

She'd finally found out exactly what sort of man he was, and hadn't liked the picture. Never again would she smile at him, tease him into laughter, give him her love as he gave her his. He'd been right about how much their parting would hurt.

He finally roused to the point of remembering he'd tossed his gun into the bushes, and went to look for it. It took a couple of minutes to find, but once he had it he turned around to see Anita arriving. She needed to hold up her ID to get herself through the crowd of deputies, but once through she came directly over to him.

"I hear you're due the giant family-size box of congratulations," she said with a grin. "You figured out what was going on, and your girlfriend figured out who. Control is delighted with your decision to work with her, and has your medal all ready and waiting. They said to tell you that you two make a great team."

"Yeah, thanks," Greg muttered, starting to turn away. Anita was talking about a team that hadn't survived, and he wasn't up to discussing it.

"What's the matter with you two?" she demanded, putting a hand to his arm to stop him. "First I see Randall on my way over here, and she looks at me, bursts out crying, then runs into her suite. Now I talk to you, and find all the welcome and affection you would get from your average wicked stepmother. What have I done? If someone kicked your puppy, it certainly wasn't me."

"Wait a minute," Greg said, turning back to frown at her. "Did you say Laine saw you and *then* started crying? She wasn't crying already?"

"Before she spotted me she didn't look happy, but she definitely wasn't crying," Anita agreed. "Is that supposed to be significant? She and I have never met, so how could it be?"

"But the two of you *were* in my room at almost the same time," Greg explained excitedly. "If she saw you and decided we had something going, she'd think I was using her. Right after you left my room was when she first began acting odd."

"You're delighted to hear she thinks you've been using her?" Anita summed up flatly, staring at him narrow-eyed. "Greg, I know you don't believe in tak-

ing vacations, but this time you've been working hard
enough to need one. As a good friend, I advise you to
think about—''

"You're absolutely right!" he interrupted with a
grin, reaching out to pull her into a brief, tight hug. "I
do need a vacation, and I know exactly who I'm going to take it with. And Anita—don't call me, I'll call
you.''

He was actually laughing as he made his way
through the herd of officials, and all Anita could do
was shake her head as she stared after him. The poor
guy had finally flipped, but he went out with a giant
win to his credit. Maybe Control would be grateful
enough to give him the time to pull himself together.
She would certainly cover for him as long as possible...

"HOW CAN YOU possibly be all right?" Bob demanded as he followed Laine into her living room. "A
minute ago you were having hysterics.''

"That wasn't hysterics," Laine denied, using the
tissue from her purse. "I was only crying a little, and
now I've stopped. First thing tomorrow, I want you to
call the people involved with the movie. If they're still
in a position to go ahead with the project even without one of their backers, tell them I've made up my
mind. If they change the location, I'll do the movie.''

"Nissa would be glad to hear you say that," Bob
told her softly. "She knew what this movie could do
for you, and she was anxious to see you accept. But
why were you crying? You looked at that very stylish
woman, had a fit, and ran. Was she wearing an outfit
you planned to wear? And even worse, in the same
color?''

"You sound ridiculous when you're being catty," Laine told him, taking off her shoes and tossing them away. "I don't have an outfit like that, not that I'd mind. It was—"

Laine's words ended abruptly when she realized what she was saying. The woman's clothes had been really good, far above the budget of even the best-paid chambermaid. And budget wasn't the only consideration...

"Bob, if you had to guess, would you think that woman was a member of the housekeeping staff?" she asked, turning to look at him. "Picture her in a uniform, and then answer."

"A uniform alone wouldn't do it," he denied without the least hesitation. "She would have to lose most of the confidence she moved with, and also that air of style. If I were casting her, it would be as almost anything else."

"And maybe one thing in particular," Laine murmured, realizing she might have made a terrible mistake. She'd forced Greg into telling her about *himself,* but she hadn't asked about other agents he might be working with. And of course he wouldn't mention it himself, not when the confidence could put a co-worker in danger. She might not have seen what she thought she had.

But that still didn't guarantee he was serious about her. Laine began pacing with the thought, forced to consider the possibility. Even if he didn't have another woman there, what proof did she have that he wasn't eager to end their association? What was there to show beyond all doubt...

"Oh, to hell with proof," she growled, stopping to point a finger at Bob. "I'm going to walk right up to him and *ask*. Isn't that better than standing around guessing?''

"If you say so," he agreed. "I don't know what *else* you said, but—"

By then Laine was no longer listening, but looking for her shoes. Why in hell hadn't she paid attention to where she was throwing them? How could she go charging off without shoes?

She found one fairly quickly, but when the second refused to turn up she wasn't going to waste any more time. Barefoot or not she had someone to find, before he disappeared out of her life. She headed resolutely for the door, threw it open, and—

—stood staring at the object of her quest. Greg himself hovered right outside the door, and the expression on his face said he'd been caught hesitating instead of knocking.

"Greg," she said, suddenly very unsure about putting her feelings into words. "Are you—did you want to see me?"

"I—uh—thought I'd make sure you remembered about talking to the sheriff tomorrow," he stumbled, not quite looking at her. "And I forgot to mention that my people will also need a statement."

"Oh—sure," Laine forced herself to say, almost more terrified than when she'd had a gun pointed at her. "Tomorrow—the sheriff and a statement for your people. Sure."

And that seemed to be the end of what they had to say to each other. Laine had acted in front of cameras, spoken to people by the hundreds in person and had even confronted actual murderers. None of it had been even a tenth as frightening as the thought of telling this man she loved him. What if it made him embarrassed rather than happy? What if—

"I have something to ask you," she blurted, hurrying before she lost the courage to speak at all. It took a moment, but then it came to her that he'd said the same exact words at almost the same time.

"What do you have to ask?" They stood there like two echoes, each one waiting for the other to start another round.

"Go ahead and ask," Laine finally ventured, but Greg just moved his head in a vague way.

"No, it's all right, *you* go ahead and ask," he countered weakly, trying to smile. "Ladies first and all that..."

"It really is about time men stood up for their rights," she returned, all but trembling with terror. "*You* go ahead..."

"Okay, that's it, I've had enough of this." The words had come from Bob, and they turned their heads in surprise to see him standing there with fists on hips. "Inside, you two, and I mean right now. If you're going to act like a couple of small children, that's the way you'll be treated. Move."

Laine wasn't in the habit of taking orders from people, but somehow she found herself in the living room. Greg was right behind her, looking just as uncomfortable as she felt. They each took one end of a couch and sat, and Bob glared back and forth between them.

"I've never seen anything like it in my life," he lectured, sounding totally out of patience. "The two of you come close enough to the Grim Reaper to shake hands with him, and all you do is shrug and grin. But when it comes time to tell each other about how you feel, you shuffle your feet, hem and haw, check the time, remember a previous appointment— For pity's sake, will you please grow up? If I leave you alone in here, do you think it will accomplish anything?''

Laine looked down at her hands, seeing out of the corner of her eye that Greg was doing almost the same. Bob didn't seem to understand how much more important than life and death this was, the discussion of real, true feelings. The thought of death was frightening, but not half as much as the possibility of going on alone, loving but not being loved back . . .

''You have fifteen minutes,'' Bob stated, checking his watch for the time. ''After that I'll be back, and if I'm not intruding, you two are in trouble.''

He gave them each a final glare and stomped out of the suite, closing the door loudly enough to leave no doubt about his departure. Laine flinched a little, and looked up to see Greg shaking his head.

''I think I'm going to wish he was involved in the murders after all,'' he said, taking a deep breath. ''Having had to listen to that lecture tempts me into considering how nice it would be to put him under arrest.''

''But at least you do know now that he's innocent?'' Laine said with a faint smile. ''The last time we discussed the point, you weren't sure at all.''

''Having him save my life did well in convincing me,'' Greg replied, matching her smile. ''If not for him, I would have been too short of breath to come charging to your rescue again. He now has a second Chinese Obligation, and the way he talked to me proves he knows it.''

''Isn't it funny what very different people can have in common?'' Laine said, feeling warm inside, but then she really heard what he'd said. ''Greg! You were almost killed? Are you sure you're all right?''

Laine reached her hand out with the question, and when Greg saw that he shifted a little closer to take it.

"No, as a matter of fact I'm not all right," he answered, all amusement gone. "Laine, I really do need to ask you—did you see Anita in my room this morning? If you did, it isn't what you think. She and I work together and are friends—like you and Bob. There's nothing else between us."

Laine was tempted to feel dizzy with relief, especially with Greg's hand holding her so tightly. But there was something else bothering him, she could see it in his eyes, and that brought back the fear.

"I believe you, and I think I'm delighted," she ventured, pushing her courage for all it was worth. "The only problem is—I don't know what the last problem is. Is it something about me, Greg? Something you can't accept?"

"You?" he echoed with a snort, releasing her hand. "How can there be anything wrong with you? You're perfect, but I—I don't quite measure up the same. It bothered you when you saw me kill Roberts, and I can't blame you for that. There are times when my job requires me to cause harm, to tempt danger, to do all sorts of unsavory things. How could I be so selfish and brutal as to want to force all that on the most wonderful woman ever born? I must have been crazy to come here and bother you..."

At that point he was no longer looking at her, and Laine was so shocked that she nearly missed it when he began to get up. But nearly doesn't count when you're prepared to move fast enough, and she was in his lap before he'd moved more than an inch.

"And where the hell do you think *you're* going?" she demanded, putting her hands to his chest. "You may be totally crazy in the head, but that doesn't mean

I'm about to let you escape. Go ahead and try it, and then see what happens.''

"Why does it sound like you're blackmailing me again?" he asked, looking bewildered. "Laine, you don't really want a man like me. You deserve so much better..."

"That's true, but you're what I've got and I'm prepared to settle," she returned with a grin. "And you'd better get used to the idea, or my report to your people on the details of this case will be very detailed indeed."

"Oh?" he said, finally looking as though he were moving back from the brink of tragedy. "What sort of details are we talking about?"

"Oh, details like the way you stood still for blackmail the first time," she said, loving the touch of his big hands on her waist. "A man who gives in so easily can't be the best of security risks, and I wouldn't be surprised if they fired you because of it."

"You're blackmailing me into keeping my job?" he demanded, one step away from outrage. "But my job is the problem here. Don't you understand—"

"Greg, don't *you* understand that job or not, you're the man I love?" she interrupted, touching his beautiful face with her hands. "You're not a horrible monster for doing what you do. Hurting people, even people who deserve it, bothers you, but you accept that ache for the sake of the good people in this world. How can that make you a monster?"

"You love me?" he asked with growing delight, as though that was all he'd heard. "I'm so crazy about you I can't even remember to breathe, and you love me back?"

"Completely," she assured him with a kiss. "Absolutely." Another kiss. "Helplessly and hopelessly.

Does this mean you're giving in to my blackmail again?"

"What choice do I have?" he asked with a laugh, wrapping her in his arms. "If I don't, I'll just get knocked down and walked on. Have I told you how wonderful you are?"

"Not nearly enough," she decided, circling him with her own arms. "But why don't you kiss me first? We can save the conversation for later."

She raised her face to him, but the kiss he gave her was as brief as hers had been.

"I have a final question before we end the conversation," he said. "I'll need to know for the marriage licence, so this isn't strictly curiosity. What's your real name?"

"My real name is Laine Randall," she answered with a grin. "My parents are intelligent people who plan ahead, so they gave me a name that would do for whatever I became. Didn't Mr. and Mrs. Williams do the same for their son Greg?"

"Ah, not exactly," he admitted with something of a shrug. "It's a long story, but the short of it is you won't be Mrs. Williams. Will that bother you?"

"Not even if it turns out to be Mrs. Hey You," Laine promised. "Do you think you can kiss me *now?*"

"I think I'd better," he said, already touching her lips with his. "We don't have much of that fifteen minutes left, and I really don't want another lecture. Just follow my lead."

"Mmm," Laine agreed, already losing herself to the wonder of loving and being loved. "Wherever you go..."

With Gentleman Greg holding her so tightly, who needed Dirty Harry?

Following the success of WITH THIS RING and
TO HAVE AND TO HOLD, Harlequin brings you

JUST MARRIED

SANDRA CANFIELD
MURIEL JENSEN
ELISE TITLE
REBECCA WINTERS

just in time for the 1993 wedding season!

Written by four of Harlequin's most popular authors, this
four-story collection celebrates the joy, excitement and
adjustment that comes with being "just married."

You won't want to miss this spring tradition, whether
you're just married or not!

AVAILABLE IN APRIL WHEREVER HARLEQUIN
BOOKS ARE SOLD